The Artist & The Assassin

# The Artist &

## THE ASSASSIN

### MARK FRUTKIN

The Porcupine's Quill

Library and Archives Canada Cataloguing in Publication

Title: The artist & the assassin / Mark Frutkin.

Other titles: Artist and the assassin

Names: Frutkin, Mark, 1948– author.

Identifiers: Canadiana (print) 20210201959 | Canadiana (ebook) 20210201967
 | ISBN 9780889848801 (softcover) | ISBN 9780889848887 (PDF)

Subjects: LCSH: Caravaggio, Michelangelo Merisi da, 1573–1610—Fiction.
 | LCGFT: Novels.

Classification: LCC PS8561.R84 A89 2021 | DDC C813/.54—dc23

1   2   3   •   23   22   21

Published by The Porcupine's Quill, 68 Main Street, PO Box 160,
Erin, Ontario NOB 1TO. http://porcupinesquill.ca

Edited by Stephanie Small. Represented in Canada by Canadian Manda. Trade orders are available from University of Toronto Press. All characters, locations, businesses, and organizations in this book are either fictitious or are used fictitiously. Any resemblance to actual people, living or dead, or to real places and organizations is a product of the author's imagination and entirely coincidental.

We acknowledge the support of the Ontario Arts Council and the Canada Council for the Arts for our publishing program. The financial support of the Government of Canada is also gratefully acknowledged.

To my wonderful and always supportive siblings:

Bud, Larry and Marilyn

'Sing to me of the man, Muse, the man of twists and turns
driven time and again off course ...'

—*The Odyssey*, Homer (translation by Robert Fagles)

# ◂⟨ THE ASSASSIN ⟩▸

---

*Rome 1600*

*I am the cloud in the sky and you, artist, the cloud's shadow scurrying over the earth. I am the cloud over your shoulder, sailing through the heavens, encountering no resistance. I carry lightly the thoughts, the belief, of a man who has never known doubt, while you, Michelangelo Merisi da Caravaggio, are the shadow of the cloud on the earth, rolling up and down hills as you try to escape. Where cloud and cloud's shadow meet will be your end.*

He has me posing as a saint, me, Luca Passarelli, with a thief for a father and my mother a wet-nurse. To be precise, he wants me playing Saint Matthew. Matthew, the one called by Christ from the streets to his spiritual life as an apostle. I sit at a table in the vaulted cellar of a palazzo belonging to one Cardinal Del Monte. I'm waiting with the artist's other models, several older louts and two young men, boys really, snappily dressed in silks, wealthy punks out slumming with the likes of us. The artist chooses to pose me as the apostle and saint. If you can imagine that. Me a saint. I would qualify for a saint's vow of poverty, certainly, but not by choice. Me with my one set of worn, flea-ridden clothing—a shirt, a tunic, and a pair of hose with holes in the knees. I cannot afford anything else. He has made me up to look older than I am. And I am no Jew, though Matthew was.

Altogether, seven of us pose in this cellar. Two of the models stand across the room, representing Jesus and Peter. Christ himself is pointing at me. The rest of us sit around the table counting the coins I gathered as if we are preparing for a night of gambling. I am the focus. Me, posing as Matthew, known as Levi the Tax Collector in the ancient stories. The light shines on me, and on the young scamp to my left, one of the artist's favourites, I hear. I wonder if he is bedding the boy? Could be. I wouldn't be surprised, but I can't say for sure.

Michelangelo Merisi, this artist from a little village called Caravaggio near Milan, stands across the room, gazing into his enormous canvas and working it, licking his brush before stabbing it again into his palette, and occasionally glancing out at us models posed around the table. His eyes are sharp, he bites his lip, he wears his thick, black hair longish in the front. Youthful style. A small window of this cellar is covered by a sheet of paper soaked in olive oil. I watched him early the first morning pour the oil over the sheet in a large pan. I could smell it. Expensive stuff. Enough oil for a family of six for a month.

The old guy sitting to my right complained on the second afternoon: 'Why not make a quick drawing and let us out of here, finish the painting in your studio?'

Merisi didn't even look up from his palette when he replied in a flat voice, 'I don't draw.'

He offered no more than that. Not, I *cannot* draw, but I *don't* draw. No explanation. No apology. Nothing. As if we were made of clay and he the Creator. What kind of artist is he then? I'm no expert, but it seems to me an artist should at least have the skill to draw.

We sit here day after day as he vanishes into that other room in his huge canvas—it must be more than ten feet across—coming out once in a while to look at us. We are statues to him. Models. Actors. Our lives disappearing, dissolving into thin air, vanishing into his great work. We are worth less than drying pigment.

'Stop moving,' he warns, when one of the boys adjusts his seat.

As long as he keeps putting coins in my pocket, I will sit here and put up with it, but I don't have to like it.

———

He is so utterly obsessive, this damned artist. It seems he has to paint every single day, every moment that light is at the window. He never takes a day off but has us in here to pose for his great work, every day for weeks on end.

Once we are seated, except for occasional short breaks, we have been warned to remain still and in place. I spend hours with my head turned as I stare at the models playing Jesus and Peter, my arm raised and aching as I point at myself as if to say in response to the summons, 'Who? Me?' I have nothing to do but listen and think. Bells, near and far, at every hour, tolling my life away. My head itching with lice to the point of madness. The wheezing, stinking, rotten-tooth breath of the old codger next to me. The gurgling of my stomach. The painter's feet as he shuffles about behind the canvas. If I shift my gaze without turning my head, I can see him at work, that is, the lower half of him, moving back and forth. When he comes to the edge of the canvas to stare out at us, his tableau, he remembers precisely where he placed each model. If anyone has moved, even shifted in his seat slightly, he screams insults and threatens not to pay any of us. Finally, when we break for lunch, I, who never pray, offer up a quick paternoster in thanks.

What he does not know—well, I am not about to tell him. Me, I am no saint, as I said. I admit to having five murders on my head. Not accidents. Not outbursts of anger or hatred. Murders I committed without shame or hesitation, murders I plotted and planned, tracking my victims for days, months even, once a year and a half. I barely knew the men I murdered, only digging into their lives enough to discover their habits, where I would find them on a dark road, when they would have their guard down. I was paid handsomely. But that money is gone—posing for this artist today will pay for tonight's meat, a gut-full of wine later, and perhaps a loaf of bread tomorrow to soak up my lingering hangover. Some saint I am.

Getting drunk is the only way I can forget the faces of the men whose throats I've slit. I said I murder willingly and without shame but their faces often return unbidden. That final look, it stays with you. But even more than getting drunk, I enjoy the hangover. I awake feeling as if my limbs are separated from my body, totally flattened, as if I spent the entire night banging my head against a stone wall (which I might have done—I don't recall). My stomach feels like a storm at sea or a pot of boiling tripe soup. I admit I love that feeling of having been purged, emptied to the core. The necessary cleansing before the road to so-called recovery—and the next bout. And the next murder too, more than likely. For there will be another. After all, it is my profession, my own art.

Business is slow. This work as a model merely fills a temporary need. I did not seek out the artist. He noticed me on the portico of the Pantheon one evening, a place I go to gamble. He said I had the 'perfect' face, said I looked like a Jew though I wore no yellow cap, offered me a good handful of coins to sit for him in his studio.

This artist, this Signor Michelangelo Merisi, can afford to pay well. The favourite of the wealthy and famous Cardinal Del Monte, he lives upstairs in the cardinal's palazzo. His fame grows as fast as mould on gutter-fruit. All Rome talks about him but, really, he's no better than me. Several nights I have come upon him lying in the street, face in a pile of horseshit, stinking of cheap wine, having pissed himself. Quick with rapier and dagger too, he is. A real temper. They say he has taken part in numerous scrapes and dust-ups. Around Piazza Navona last week again. Insults the other artists. Most of them, anyway. Crazy.

I wonder if they feel much different in the hand: dagger and brush, brush and stiletto. Plunge into pigment, stab into canvas. Thrust your sword into your enemies, those saints and monsters. For a startling bright red, for a warm and brilliant scarlet, nothing better than to dip your brush into the boiling pot of a still beating heart ...

The other evening on the street, I saw him talking to a young girl, running his hand over her black velvet sleeve as he roiled in the pleasure of the sumptuous cloth. I watched as he let his hand slide further up her arm, pretending to enjoy the cloth until he was stroking the soft flesh of her shoulder and neck. She barely noticed, believing he was still feeling the velvet nap. But it was the skin he was after, and it was her smooth, white skin he got. I watched from a distance. Too young to know any better, that girl. Probably about fourteen, and she works the streets. I see her out, not every night but once in a while. Why? Likely because she has to eat. Hunger is like that—fill the belly first, then worry later about sin and salvation. But I hate this Merisi. So arrogant, so full of himself. And I hate myself even more for not spilling his guts right there and then. But I need his coins.

Now he has dressed me for my role. Now I am the one in black velvet, as if I, Luca Passarelli, professional assassin, am a two-bit actor playing a saint or a gentleman with a floppy hat.

———————

He titled the painting, *The Calling of Saint Matthew*. I am being 'called' all right—but not for any saintly or Christian duties. I know he saw himself as Jesus in that work. What a strange premonition. Jesus calls to me in the painting. *Come follow me, Levi.* I try to resist, pointing to the old fellow next to me. *You mean him? You want him? No,* Jesus says. *I want you. Come follow me, Matthew, follow me into the world with your new name and your new life.*

———————

A few days later, I hurry in the direction of the Ponte Sant'Angelo on my way to another day of unbearable tedium in Merisi's studio. As I place my foot on the bridge, I see that the executioner has been busy since dawn. Five fresh heads are mounted on posts on each side, flies at their eyes. The heads stare straight ahead, shocked at finding themselves suddenly dead. I have seen plenty of dead men in my day. I'm no saint. I have seen the faces of the men I've killed—I felt no hate for them. But they were grown men with blackened hearts and I simply needed the money.

Oftentimes, like today, I have passed the heads of the executed mounted on Ponte Sant'Angelo set out by the authorities as examples and warnings for those of us who might consider a life of crime. I usually pass by with barely a glance at the poor buggers, but this time I stop in my tracks. The fifth head on the right—I know him. We worked together on several murders. Enzo Rondini. Not an easy fellow. Always angry, he could turn on an accomplice in an instant. The fact that he had to slit a throat here and there in order to eat did not bother him, or me. In his youth, he had his ear cut off by the authorities for a long-forgotten crime. We live in hard times.

I stop and stare. That could be me up there. Probably will be someday. Well, we've all got to die, haven't we?

I gaze at his head, gore still oozing from the neck, and an odd and unexpected thought comes to me—how would he paint it, this severed head? How would the artist present the look on Enzo's face? What do I care how he'd paint it? But we cannot always control the thoughts that tumble into our brains when staring at the severed head of an old friend. I shrug and walk on, crossing the Piazza Rusticucci, a dull square with a trickling fountain in the middle and a trough for animals at one end. The image of Enzo's severed head still flows heavily through me like the nearby noxious waters of the Tiber.

Later, in the cellar of the cardinal's palazzo where I model and Merisi paints me as Saint Matthew, the artist shouts at me. 'What is wrong with you today!?' He leans out from behind his canvas, eyes bugged out. 'The look on your face, it's all wrong! I have told you over and over, I want a look of surprise and expectancy and confusion. Not this visage of despair and sadness. Get out, I cannot work with you today. Get out! Everyone, get out!'

On my return from that accursed studio, I stop again on the bridge to see Rondini. I call him my friend but that is far from the truth. We were accomplices but that's all. The flies still busy themselves about his eyes and now maggots writhe in the gore oozing from his neck. Rondini does not look happy to be here.

I glance over the bridge's parapet and notice three fishermen beside the Tiber, which is lined with low banks of garbage and refuse. A dead horse goes floating by as the fishermen are lifting a floppy sturgeon from their boat. *Fish-head soup.* The thought assails me. *I want fish-head soup.* But before I turn away to hurry to the tavern for soup I can afford, I take one last glance at Rondini the thief, the murderer.

Again, the question comes unbidden into my skull—*How would the artist paint Rondini's severed head?* I recall as I left the studio earlier, I happened to glance over my shoulder at his canvas and thought, *If beauty exists at all in this world of misery, this is it.*

Standing on the bridge now, staring at Enzo's head, the Tiber flowing beneath me, I wonder how it is that this arrogant pig of an artist makes me see the world through his eyes. I am angry. Angry for being dismissed by Merisi. Angry because I can barely find a way to fill my belly. Angry because the world is thick with misery and pain. I look again at the severed head of my so-called friend, stare into his eyes, and realize that at the heart of anger is profound sadness.

But I am no philosopher so the thought doesn't stick.

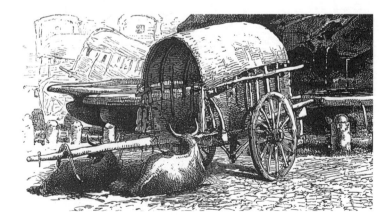

# ⊰ THE ARTIST ⊱

---

*I'm running along a beach under a scorching sun, my feet so heavy in the sand I can barely lift them. I keep turning my head around, looking back, searching for the assassin. Is he there, is he still pursuing me? I'm not sure. . . . The heat is unbearable. The sea is no relief. It is molten, glowing lead, waves heaving, painfully bright. The landscape is a fever dream. My entire life, a fever dream. My eyes sting and burn; sweat runs into them. My clothing is soaked, the sun relentless. I can feel my heart pounding in my head like an iron bell that, though struck, refuses to ring. I am burning up with fever, the sun unyielding, the light, the light. . .*

---

*1582, the village of Caravaggio in Lombardy*

What he remembers most from that day during his childhood is the small lizard unnaturally still above her bed, awaiting the inevitable.

After the day's work in the fields, the boy leaves his uncle's stone farmhouse and walks through the twisting alleys of the village, returning to his own dwelling where he knows his mother is dying. He doesn't even remember his father, gone so long.

The village resembles a stone hive. Houses no more than cells of rock, each abutting the next. Arches of granite over low entryways that descend to deep cellars. *My mother is dying.* Narrow steps of stone lead up to cracked and blackened wooden doors. Uneven cobbles pave the streets. Everything looks the same, cobbles cut of the same rock as the walls. No greenery, no gardens, no vines, just stone. *My mother is dying.*

When the boy gains a view to the intense afternoon glare at the end of an alley, he glimpses green fields stretching away in the distance, a few chestnut copses here and there, a line of Lombardy poplars to mark the edge of a farm. He shades his eyes and looks up. The fierce sun still beats down on roof tiles that ripple with light.

As he enters the village's cramped piazza, a cat's-cradle of swallows swings in the air high above. He notes the campanile next to the church, the hands of its clockface stuck at three o'clock. It has not worked for years. His mother used to tell him that the clock stopped the day he was born, as if his birth, by the grace of God, were a miraculous event. He doubts it is true.

He enters an alley, one wall lit by sunlight. *My mother is dying.* The unlit wall on the other side is dull, in uniform shadow. He turns back to the wall touched by the sun and sees how it comes alive, glittering and glowing with colour. *My mother is dying.*

He climbs twelve worn steps and stops at the door before his mother's house, his house. A shaft of sunlight strikes the old wood of the door, deepening the blacks, illuminating the yellow. He enters and is surrounded by shadow. From the doorway, he squints into the dark. Across the room his mother sleeps in her bed. He sees that she wakes and turns toward him as he approaches. 'Momma.'

Her lips are dry and cracked and bloodless. On the wall behind her, a small green lizard watches, motionless and alert. It seems to him as if the lizard is waiting for her soul to exit her body so he can gobble it up.

Her eyelids lift and she holds out her hand. 'Ah, my beautiful child,' she whispers. He takes her hand in his and sits on a stool beside the bed. A rancid smell saturates the room and he notices again the yellowness of her skin, the touch of green in the bags under her eyes, the sag of her narrow breasts under the blanket. 'I had a dream,' she says.

Still holding her hand, he leans against the bed and listens. 'I was staring into a pool of water.' The words come in whispers from her lips, interspersed with breathy gasps. 'I could see … my face in the water. It was rising toward me as … as I was falling into it. I was about to drown in my own reflection, to fall into that watery mirror.' She pauses, punctuates with a small cough. 'All evens out in the end, my beautiful son. Everything in balance. Whatever you take in life you give back in death.' She looks up into his eyes. 'Eleven years ago, I gave birth to you. Like me, you were born … under the sign of the Scales. All comes even in the end.' She pauses. 'Pass me my Bible.'

Continuing to grip her hand, he finds the small Bible on a nearby bench and hands it to her. Not many in their village are able to read but she can and therefore he can too. She simply holds the Bible in her hand, doesn't open it.

He lets go of her hand and rests it on the blanket. 'I don't want to be a farmer. You know I long to be an artist.'

She blinks, speaking slowly. 'You find it difficult … working for your uncle?'

'Yes. This afternoon, he was ploughing. I was to walk behind and plant bean seeds. But I noticed the soil was different colours in different rows so I knelt and examined the earth.' He grows excited, talking quickly. 'I called uncle over and showed him how in some places the soil was brown, in others black, in others still it was lighter as if it had yellow in it. I also showed him soil that had specks of silver or gold like on the stones of the village walls.'

'And what did my brother say?'

'He said it's just soil. Good for growing root vegetables or sometimes leafy vegetables, or not good for growing anything. He told me to stop wasting time. He showed no interest in the colours.'

'Teodoro is a farmer, my son. And he loves it. But you do not have to be the same.' She lifts her hand and runs it through his curly, black hair. By the time he looks up, she has fallen back asleep.

———

The local priest, Don Bartolomeo, was a frequent visitor at the farmhouse of Uncle Teodoro and, one day, noticed a painting on the wall. 'By the boy?' he asked.

Teodoro nodded.

The padre said to Teodoro, 'It's unusually good work. Next week I am going to Venice to visit my sister. Would you like me to purchase pigments for the boy, and some good canvas? He has a God-given talent that should be nurtured.'

Teodoro's first impulse was to reply that the orphaned boy would be a farmer like himself, but he hesitated. He had quickly discovered that the boy had no interest in working on the land or with animals. Perhaps his natural talent would prove to be useful for the boy's future. So, he agreed.

As soon as the boy received the priest's package from the colour sellers in Venice, he immediately set to work in his room.

A few days later, he was excited to show Teodoro what he had discovered. 'Look, Uncle, this lead white pigment, I can see a reddish-yellow ghost in it. Do you see it?'

Teodoro stared at the blotch of pigment on the canvas. He saw nothing but white there but he did not want to disappoint the boy so he wagged his head from side to side as if to agree without really agreeing.

'And look at this,' the boy exclaimed. '*Ocra gialla*, it's called. This yellow pigment comes all the way from Cyprus.'

'Ah, that is why it was so expensive.'

'And for black, Don Bartolomeo said the seller of pigments in Venice told him I can use soot from our lamps, or I can even burn some dried grape vines.'

Teodoro nodded, unimpressed but not wishing to squelch the boy's enthusiasm.

'And look at this, if I add a bit of this lead-tin yellow to some green and ochre, I can paint the grass of the fields and the leaves on the trees. Do they not look like real foliage?'

Teodoro patted the boy on the head. 'Yes, yes, real leaves, indeed. Just like the ones on the trees out there. Well done.'

---

The boy was sleepless, and energized as a young horse. He recalled that a few days before, a master painter from Milan, Simone Peterzano, had passed through their village looking for apprentices. Don Bartolomeo had brought the Master to the uncle's farm where he knew the young Michelangelo Merisi had gained something of a local reputation for his ability to draw and paint. He and his uncle had met with the Master to discuss a possible apprenticeship. The Master's gaze frightened him. He had sad, angry eyes to go along with a perpetual frown. The boy thought he had the look of a mean dog. When the padre brought the Master to Teodoro's house, they all sat at the kitchen table and Teodoro poured glasses of red wine for the priest and the Master. 'From grapes grown in my own vineyard,' the uncle pointed out. Peterzano winced when he took a drink of the wine and let it sit for the rest of the visit.

The Master announced, 'I was a student of the famous Tiziano Vecelli in Venice. The boy could not possibly find a better tutor in the art of painting than myself.' The boy had no idea who Tiziano Vecelli was and was sure his uncle was in the dark as well, but neither of them opened their mouths.

'All right, set out some of your pictures. I only wish to see the very best ones. I don't have all day to spend looking at childish pictures. How many good ones have you?'

'Six.' The boy noted that the Master had said 'pictures', not 'paintings', as if it gave him a bad taste in his mouth.

One by one, he placed the paintings on the table. The Master gave each a quick, cursory glance and then motioned to see the next.

The Master sat back, noticed the glass of wine still full before him, almost reached for it, then decided against it and smirked. 'Your painting in oils shows a serious lack of skill. You still have much to learn. Never mind about colour,' he added, 'find the line first, simply find the line. You must learn to draw with precision.' He turned to Teodoro. 'I am likely making a serious mistake but I will be willing to take the boy on as an apprentice, if you have the means.'

'I will find the money,' Teodoro said.

But Michele seethed over Peterzano's tepid comments. *The Master knows nothing. Find the line! Why, when the world is filled to bursting with colour?*

———————

The next day, after his chores are done, late in the afternoon, the boy takes a walk along the edge of the deep forest at the far side of his uncle's fields. He feels the bulge of rounded stones in his pocket and one stone cool in his hand. He hopes to bring back a few small birds that his uncle can roast that evening to add to their meal.

No birds seem to be about. He stops and gazes into the forest which is thick with trees of all kinds: spruce, pine, oak, chestnut. Deep in the gloom of the wood, something catches his eye. There, in the darkest core of the forest, the shadows at their blackest, he sees a beam of sunlight that penetrates the branches and ignites a patch of leaves near the forest floor. The slash of sunlight brings the patch alive. The illuminated leaves possess a clarity that he realizes is impossible without the surrounding dark. He starts considering which colours and pigments he can use to bring out the patch of light to its fullest effect.

Turning, he looks back across the field. The sky is full of late-afternoon sunlight but lacks the brilliance of the patch of leaves in the forest.

Just then, a large crow bursts from the forest edge into the air. The bird flies low above his head and he notices that its shadow passes right along the ground and over him. *The bird and its shadow are separate,* he thinks, *but they are one.*

He hurries back to his uncle's farmyard. He is excited to try to paint the vibrant patch of leaves.

————————

*Three years later, Milan*

Every day, the apprentices practise drawing draperies from a wooden model that has been covered with fabric dipped in wet plaster and allowed to dry. Or they work from live models, always old, naked men. Or they paint angels, endless angels—ethereal and light as cirrus skies, copying them badly from poorly done originals.

Michele is bored beyond belief and waits in fevered anticipation for those few times when he is left alone in the studio while the others are off on some project or other. Today he is alone and happy to be so.

A blaze of sunlight through the window illumines a marble mortar and pestle filled with chunks of unground lapis lazuli to be ground into ultramarine pigment. From across the studio, Michele stares at it. He appreciates the way the light strikes one side of the mortar, shines from its lip, and travels up the thick handle of the pestle. He approaches and stares at the lumps of lapis lazuli in the bowl, delighting in the sumptuous blue colour, with bits of gold and a single, narrow white vein in the largest piece.

Master Peterzano can afford to buy precious and expensive pigments from Florence, Venice and distant Holland. He keeps the costly lapis lazuli in a secret hiding place in the studio. While all the apprentices were busy that morning, the Master removed some of the stones and placed them in the mortar. Michele saw him do it. Then the Master left with the other apprentices for a nearby church in Milan to spend the afternoon preparing the walls for a commission, a fresco depicting the dead Christ's removal from the cross. The Master instructed Michele to stay back and spend his day grinding the blue pigment. Before leaving, he explained in his annoyingly precise way, speaking slowly as if Michele were half-idiot. 'Lapis lazuli must be ground for hours to attain the correct consistency. Like all pigments, the finer it is, the better it will be for painting. So, keep at it. I want you to spend the entire day grinding it. Do not disappoint me.'

Michele wondered if this was a test. If the Master expected him to steal the valuable lapis lazuli and run off with it. With a sinking heart, he glowers at the mortar and pestle. He hates grinding pigments. In fact, his own experiments with pigments have proved to him that a finer grind does not always make for better colours. In fact, one day he tried mixing a ground pigment with one that was less fine. Like today, everyone was gone, he had been left behind again, to grind away. He decided to test his pigment in a painting. He discovered that the pigment still contained tiny crystals that awoke more brilliant colours when the light struck the canvas. But he has no experience with lapis lazuli. He decides he will start the grinding later. He wants to try copying one of the Master's landscapes.

After he has painted for several hours, enchanted by the smell of the oil and the brilliance of the pigments, he loses track of the time in his creative fervour. Suddenly the Master returns alone, unexpectedly early, and strides into the studio. He stops and stares. 'Michele, what in damnation are you doing!?' Michele stands, his brush poised in the air. He makes no reply. It is obvious what he is doing.

No longer a child, not quite a man, Michele is slight, thin, a good foot shorter than the Master who stands pointing at the canvas that he has been working on. To paint freely brings the boy profound joy, feeling the colours flow from his brush onto the canvas. That is his mistake—remembering the delight he took in working the colours in and out of each other, vermilion, sienna, greens of grass and pine, azure blue. He pauses, with fondness gazes at his painting, and smiles to himself. He knows that Master Peterzano is about to compliment him on his effort, is about to express how pleased he is that Michele, his best apprentice, has taken the initiative and produced a fine work of art.

*Crack!* The Master's hand catches him on the side of the head, sends him flying across the room into the stone wall.

'You dare to waste my pigments! You dare to disobey me!'

The Master strides across the room, intent, and smacks the boy down again even as he tries to stand. Then he kicks him in the stomach. The breath flies out of Michele and he feels the heavy boot again, this time in his mouth. He sees two of his teeth on the floor. Blood gushes. He curls up like a worm, trying to protect his head, as the Master kicks him again and again. This explosion has been coming for months and now that it has arrived, nothing can control or stop it.

The Master shouts through gritted teeth. 'You never listen! I promised your uncle to take you on as an apprentice and you do nothing but disobey me! You little fool! I will teach you not to waste my pigments, *my* canvas, *my* time!'

Still, Peterzano kicks him. The boy glances up and sees the strange look on the Master's face—a terrible grin that reveals his teeth, eyes livid and glowing.

Finally, the Master is spent and lurches out the door of the studio. Michele lies still, throbbing in pain, his mouth broken and bloody. With effort, groaning, he sits up, head sagging, a string of bloody drool hanging from his mouth. He pushes himself up and stands, unsteady, gazing about the room. Limping across the studio, he stops and stares at the Master's own most recent painting on its easel—his 'finest work', the Master called it, a painting that he has laboured over for two months, a portrait of the local bishop. The boy knocks it to the floor and straddles the canvas. Unbuttoning his trousers, he pisses on it.

———————

Strangely, during his beating by the Master, while his guts were awash with fear, another part of his being was elsewhere. From his position lying on the floor, he had glanced up at the madman kicking him. *What a fascinating angle,* he had thought, *a unique perspective: the large*

*foot, close up; the tapering, kinked leg; the other leg fixed like a post and holding all the weight; the lean and twist of his torso; the small head in the distance, a corner of the ceiling behind it like the inside of a pyramid. All in a foreshortened style,* di sotto in su, *'from below upwards'.* And then the pain had rushed in, overwhelming him, and he folded his arms tighter around his head. Afterwards, he never forgot that unusual perspective, as if Christ on his cross, being nailed hand and foot, was about to be lifted into position, from the horizontal to the vertical, as if Christ caught close up the swing of the hammer against blue sky, the crooked arm, the impassive face of the Roman soldier above him. The soldier's lack of passion, his ordinary look, made it seem that this was nothing special, just another crucifixion in a long history of death, just another beating at the hand of a Master, as if it had to be, it was fated that he be punished. It was fate following its own dictates, the way water from a spring has to flow downhill, the way blood must run down an arm, must drip off fingers into the thirsty earth.

———

One day in the studio, Master Peterzano, with no commissions in the offing, allows the apprentices to work on their own paintings. As he tours the room watching his half-dozen apprentices trying to impress him, he pulls up short behind Michele and says, 'I notice you have always refused to draw, Michele, but start splashing paint right on the canvas. Why is this? Drawing is the essence of painting. You will end up like that idiot Venetian, Giorgione.'

Michele holds his brush in the air a moment and turns to the Master, throws back his shoulders and stands taller. 'Drawing is not the essence of painting,' he replies, daring to disagree. 'I believe that colour is the essence of painting, not drawing. Colour and light.' He ducks to avoid the slap he sees coming and runs from the room.

------

*One year later, Rome*

'Bread! Bread! Bread!' the crowd in the square shouts.

Michele stands in an immense sea of Romans on Saint Peter's Square in the heart of the city. The Pope himself appears at his window and starts speaking to the audience but his words are drowned out by the crowd's shouts.

Michele joins in. 'Bread! Bread! Bread!'

Over the past few years, the harvests in the surrounding countryside have been inconsistent. The Papal authorities allot a ration of bread to the poor but it is never enough.

Cutpurses slink through the crowd on the square, hoping to steal what little the poor have left. Michele picks them out with ease.

If truth be told, Michele is better off than many. His Uncle Ludovico, the priest, introduced him to Monsignor Pucci who manages a wealthy household in the city. Pucci offered the young artist a room in the cellar in return for running errands, hunting rats in the palazzo, and emptying chamber pots. In return, Pucci's kitchen keeps Michele fed, but the cook has been ordered to offer him nothing but greens. Greens for breakfast, lunch, and dinner, sometimes cooked, often raw.

Michele would rather stand in the square shouting for bread than head back to be humiliated again by the man he has dubbed 'Monsignor Salad'. This very night, he decides, he will collect the two small canvases he has been working on in the cellar and leave for good. His new friend, Francesco, has offered to share a place with him—a hovel, really. But Michele sold his first painting a few days before—a picture of a boy peeling an apple—and he now has the necessary coins to make it barely possible.

'Bread!' the crowd howls. 'Bread! Bread!' The Holy Father gives up, tosses off a blessing, and scuttles back into his chambers.

Michele turns away and heads back to his cellar.

On entering his cellar, where he both sleeps and works on his paintings, Michele eyes his current canvas, a still life of red grapes and flowers. He had stolen the grapes and the white carnations early that morning from a small vineyard and garden on the grounds of an estate in the Monte Mario section of the city. After sneaking into the garden, he had slipped back over the stone wall with the grapes and flowers in a wicker basket he carried which now sits in his room. He begins to work on the painting again.

Several hours later, he pauses, grunts and flings his brush across the room. 'I will never get it right!' he shouts. Snatching up the basket of fruit and flowers, he throws it hard against the wall, snatches his stiletto off the worktable and, in a frenzy, slashes the painting into ribbons. He flees from the room and runs along the street, running and running until he is bent over, panting, gasping for breath. He realizes he is on the Ponte Sant'Angelo. Walking to the balustrade, he looks down into the Tiber. He sees a fisherman in a faded red shirt, a patch of misty red reflected in the water. The colour strikes him. 'That's it! That is the colour I want.' He hurries back to his cellar, cleans up the mess, prepares a new canvas and begins work anew.

### ❧ THE ASSASSIN ❧

I learn from my friend, Giovanni, a young, strapping lad, that the infamous heretic, Giordano Bruno, will be burned at the stake after morning prayers on the spacious Campo dei Fiori. Bruno will be brought there in a cart from San Ursula prison. Giovanni has found us some work. He and I are to accompany the cart, walking alongside to help ensure the crowds do not become unruly and attack the heretic, thus denying the flames their feast and the crowd in the campo its entertainment.

I leave my dwelling before dawn, hurrying in the dark through the sharp, penetrating cold to the prison of San Ursula. Arriving at the wide gates that mark the entrance, I join the waiting Giovanni who tears off a hunk of bread from a loaf and hands it to me, takes a piece for himself, and stuffs the rest of the loaf into his coat. After chewing in silence for a while, we hear the cart rattling over the cobbles, the clack of the horses' hooves. A small crowd has gathered in the chill and the onlookers crane their necks to see the infamous Bruno.

In the half-light, I can see the prisoner standing in the middle of the cart. His arms and legs have been tied with chains. He is a small man, thin as a blade, with stiff black hair. He stands straight, unbowed, his proud, resolute face marked with wounds and scars. On each side of him wait two priests in long robes, members of the brotherhood whose role it is to comfort the condemned. They take turns mumbling to him but the heretic ignores them, a stubborn look fixed upon his face. Two soldiers with pikes stand on the cart, four walk in front, four more follow behind.

Bruno wears a white robe to his ankles emblazoned with a large X on the front. In the rising light, we can see that red devils with forked tails dance in the flames around the X. As the cart shifts forward, Giovanni nods to the captain of the guards and he and I join in the procession, walking beside the cart.

The route to Campo dei Fiori is filling up with crowds who mock the prisoner, shouting slurs at him. To my surprise, the heretic is not the least bit meek and resigned to these attacks, but shouts back. But he does not deride them for being ignorant. Instead, he yells things I do not understand, though the friars beside him on the cart try to stop him from responding. Bruno simply moves his head about to free his mouth from their hands. He cries out, 'It may be that you fear more to deliver judgment upon me than I fear judgment.'

I turn to look up at the madman and he stares directly at me, declaring in a great voice, 'One soul can animate two bodies!' This infuriates the onlookers who threaten to attack him upon the cart, drag him down, and tear him to pieces. When a young man tries to leap aboard the cart, I see my friend Giovanni down him by knocking him in the throat, and then I have my own hands full with the crowd surging in on me. I push and shove and the guards leap into the mob swinging their pikes.

Once the throng has been beaten back, the captain orders the cart driver to halt and motions to three jailers behind, who, stepping on the spokes of the wheels, climb into the cart. Two of the jailers hold the condemned man's head still while the third, with powerful precision, shoves a long, sharp spike through one cheek and out the other, ensuring that he pierces the back of the heretic's tongue on its way. Bruno moans and gags as blood spurts on the hands of the jailer and over the condemned man's white robe. Then the jailer tugs the tip of Bruno's tongue out between his lips and thrusts another spike straight down to fasten the lips together, the tongue between them, the two spikes forming an unholy cross. The crowd roars its satisfaction and delight.

Now that the heretic has been silenced, the cart rolls on.

Soon the procession enters the campo where the massive crowd lets out a roar that sounds like long, crumpling thunder. The mob parts to let the soldiers, the jailers, the cart, as well as Giovanni and me, through to the centre of the square where wood and branches have been piled and a thick wooden stake stands tall and straight. Bruno is brought down from the cart by two soldiers and led to the stake where he is tied. The soldiers pile the branches around him as high as his chin. The crowd grows silent, awaiting the first spark of flame.

Giovanni and I stand not far from the heretic, in the first row of spectators. Next to me a young monk, with a pig's nose and wearing filthy robes, spits out, to no one in particular: 'Suffer now, Bruno, for your madness, for your blasphemous heresies!'

I turn to the monk. 'What did he believe, this man, that he should suffer and be tortured in this way?'

He replies, 'The heretic believed that the soul is in the whole body, in the bones, the blood, the heart. Is it not absurd?'

'I wouldn't know. I have always had trouble finding my soul.'

The monk gives me a look at once curious and confused, as well as distrustful. 'For his sin of pride, be assured, his body will burn like any other.'

'Aye, no doubt.'

A soldier approaches carrying a torch. He touches it to the dry branches around Bruno's feet, the mob cheers in unison, and a single tongue of flame, as if reaching up out of Hell, licks the branches above it. The fire grows, pulsing with heat. It looks like a bull with horns of flame, mounting the heretic. I look at Bruno's face. His eyes bore through me. I see no fear there. Stubborn pride, yes. But no fear. The morning breeze whips a thin banner of pure white smoke through the crowd, children run as close to the fire as they dare and throw small sticks at the heretic. The smell of his burning flesh, while disgusting, reminds me of how hungry I am. As soon as we receive our payment, I will head to the nearest tavern to eat and drink my fill. Then off to the nearest brothel.

I hear his skin crackle and his fat sizzle. He lets out a single long moan.

After the first blaze, the fire puts out little smoke. Giovanni has told me that the guards would have arranged for damp wood to be added to the pile, if they had wanted the heretic to suffer less, ensuring that he choke to death from the smoke long before feeling the raw searing of the flames. But here the wood is dry and burns white hot.

With the gathered crowd enjoying the ritual, it resembles a Mass.

But here, Bruno is both the priest who celebrates the Mass and the victim, the sacrifice, offered up to God.

I look at him again. The fire is alive still. The man is gone.

Finally, the fire fades and the crowd begins to disperse, as if disappointed there was no more excitement to be had from this sacrifice, as if they have been let down by Bruno dying so easily. Giovanni and I have been told to wait until the end. We have more work to do before the captain will give us our payment.

At last, the square has emptied out except for a few children still trying to revive the fire with their sticks. A soldier shoos them away, reaches into the hot ashes with a long hook and pulls out the skull and bones of what was once Giordano Bruno. As the bones cool on the cobbles, another soldier brings two heavy iron hammers to me and Giovanni. We take to the task of pounding Giordano Bruno's bones into powder, right on the spot. The powder and bits of bone will be taken in wooden buckets by cart to a distant fallow field and dumped there among the stones and weeds.

As I work, the powdery dust floats up into my nostrils. It seems like a ghost entering me. I wonder if Bruno's soul can take root in my chest. By the time Giovanni and I have finished we look like old men with grey hair. But I care not. I have my coins and hurry off with Giovanni to fill my belly. As we exit the square, I notice a slight cough and I wonder if Bruno has planted himself inside me. But I ignore the strange thought. Hopefully we'll make it to our favourite bordello before we fall down drunk.

## ⊰ THE ARTIST ⊱

---

Walking through the theatre of shadows that is the city at dusk, Michele is returning to his dwelling near the Ortaccio quarter into which the new Pope, Clement VIII, in his crackdown on licentiousness, has forced all Roman prostitutes to move. Michele and his friend, Francesco, parted ways as soon as Michele had sold a few more paintings and had the money to afford his own place. His shoulders hunched, Michele is tired from a day of painting apples, roses, lilies and plums, peaches, mums, asters, violets, geraniums and more plums, fruit and flowers, fruit and flowers, fruit and flowers, for a few scudi each, in the workshop of Giuseppe Cesari. The colours swim in a muddy swirl before his eyes. He often has no energy left afterwards to return to his own painting, and his taste for colour is ruined, a swamp of runny pigments. He is hungry too. The few coins in his pocket are insufficient to make both whoring and drinking tonight possible so he will have to choose one or the other. Recently he spent his few extra coins on a suit of black velvet corduroy, a suit that is already stinking with his sweat. His stomach might be drumming with emptiness much of the time, but he wants to ensure he cuts the right figure in the world of artists that he longs to enter. He is sure, without a doubt, that he can make a success of himself and the essence of being successful, he knows, is looking the part.

Michele has grown sick of doing the repetitive work that Cesari assigns him. He is an assistant and not an apprentice, yet Cesari treats him like a novice. He suspects that Cesari fears that Michele is a painter who could outshine him if given half a chance. Michele knows he can certainly outwork him, as Cesari is far more concerned about garnering his next commission than completing the previous one.

As he walks, Michele hears faint shouts of an argument echo from the half-shadows of the next square in the squalid neighbourhood. He quickens his step, wide awake now, heart starting to beat faster. But he is not running away from the fight, he's running towards it. He knows he needs the excitement of brawling to keep him going. Perhaps he can join in the fight. In his area, as often as not, the ruffians will be poor artists like him, apprentices, lowlifes who can paint a chrysanthemum if required and in the next moment go at an enemy with a stiletto. He would not mind beating the face of someone, anyone, joining the others in venting his anger at having only one suit of fine clothing, sick to death of being poor, and unaccepted and unappreciated by his contemporaries as well as those who are established players in the city's art circles. He has the sudden thought that, whatever face he is beating, it will instantly turn into Cesari's.

As he draws near, he hears the raised voices of a crowd of young men. It still sounds like a joking, teasing, slightly drunk sort of dispute. One older artist he knows is there, Onorio Longhi with his head on fire. Michele likes this artist with his blaze of red hair. He and several of his apprentices are mocking another artist Michele does not recognize, who shouts back with a gang of his own friends. Someone gets shoved and falls against a wall. The two groups rush at each other and start pounding. A moment later, rapiers are drawn.

'What happened?' Michele asks an old fellow with watery eyes, standing back in the shadows, watching.

'These artists, so easily insulted. They were in a heated discussion about who was the better painter. Every week these fights break out. Stupid young fools.'

As Michele watches the struggle, it rises to a new level of ferocity. Two toughs have a third on the cobbles and are delivering a volley of blows to his bloody face with their fists. Another three aim hard kicks to a supine figure on the ground who has stopped moving, his sword fallen aside. Michele sees by the flash of red that it is Onorio on the ground. Michele draws his rapier and leaps into the fight. The others see him coming and dodge out of the way. Onorio struggles up, wiping his face. He nods a quick thanks to Michele, picks up his sword and runs at the others.

A moment later, Michele hears the Capitoline police approaching down a street at the far side of the square. With that, the fight ends and half the crowd scurries down an alley and disappears. Michele too flees down a nearby lane, away from the police.

————————

Several days later, Michele passes Onorio Longhi in the street.

'Ah, I know you,' says the red-headed painter in greeting. 'You came to help us in that scrape the other night, yes?'

'Yes, I cannot deny it.'

'By the grace of God, I owe you a drink, at least.'

They slip into a nearby tavern and order a pot of wine and proceed to talk. Michele tells him that he too is a painter, from Lombardy, fairly new to Rome. 'I came because my uncle lives here and I thought he could assist me in getting settled and established, but as a priest he is poorer than I am.'

'What is your name? Perhaps I have heard of your work.'

'Michelangelo Merisi.'

'Michelangelo? A most unfortunate name for a painter. It's already taken.'

'That is true. My friends call me Michele. At any rate, I have work with Giuseppe Cesari, but I grow mad with boredom. I paint and paint and paint, nothing but flowers and fruit, but after working all day, I have little time left for my own canvases.'

'Cesari? An idiot of the first order. Get away as fast as you can.'

'I will, soon. In the meantime, at least he pays on schedule and I can fill my belly and buy a few paints.'

They drink and Onorio looks out the window. 'Why did you come to our aid the other night?'

'Because I believe I am much like you. I love a good fight. And I have seen several of your paintings and considered them well done. I like fighting even more than a pot of wine and a night with a beautiful young woman.'

'Listen, would you like to come along with me tonight to the tennis courts near Palazzo Firenze? It can be a good place to meet artists and, more importantly, the local aristocrats like to come there and place bets on the games and slum with us artist-types. I have picked up more than one commission there. Perhaps we will find ourselves in the wolf's mouth, as my old father used to say.' To Michele's questioning look he explains, 'It's a Roman saying. It means we will be lucky.'

'And maybe we will see those *bastardi* you were fighting with.'

'I wish it so.' Onorio nods.

They go together that evening to the courts. The gang from the previous night does not show but the trip isn't entirely wasted. Onorio introduces the young painter to a number of artists of repute in Rome, as well as a handful of wealthy men who Michele figures he would like to know better, as they are the ones who have the money and the influence to make his reputation.

———————

A week later, Michele goes with Cesari to visit a cardinal who has commissioned a painting from Cesari's studio. On the way to the cardinal's palazzo, Cesari explains to Michele: 'Cardinal Del Monte is a most learned and educated man. He comes from Florence and is able to read Latin, of course, as well as Hebrew, Greek, and several other languages, including German and Dutch. He appears to have an interest in everything: art, music, science. It is even rumoured that he dabbles in forbidden alchemy. His palace contains a number of workshops, where he and his associates can pursue various interests: clock-making, the construction of musical instruments, and so on. He is a most unusual and genial cardinal. It would be good if you held your tongue in the presence of this august man. Let me do the talking.'

The young painter doesn't trust Cesari. He recalls the old saying, 'Before you can truly know a man, you have to eat a bushel of salt with him.' He believes even if he did eat a bushel of salt with Cesari, he would still distrust him.

A servant leads them up wide stairs to the *piano nobile* level of the palace and ushers them into the presence of two cardinals who are seated in Del Monte's study. Michele notes the room has high windows with real glass in them, not simply wooden shutters. The wood-panelled room is simply, yet elegantly, furnished: two chairs only—the ones in which the prelates sit—and a heavy desk of dark wood on one side. On the desk, a stack of three leather-bound books, an inkwell, and a brass candleholder with a fresh ivory-coloured candle inserted. And, somewhat incongruously, a little terracotta dog sitting on a silk cushion. Across the room, before a crucifix on the wall, a prie-dieu with tortoise-shell columns and a leather-padded kneeler. On the wall a tapestry depicts what appears to Michele as an imaginary scene of Jerusalem: a domed church, a winding road, a hill.

The two prelates, in scarlet cassocks, their arms resting on the high armrests of their chairs of red velvet, look supremely confident. According to tradition, both visitors place a perfunctory kiss on the gold ring of each cardinal.

Michele places the painting on an easel where the cardinals can consider it. His Eminence Cardinal Del Monte is seemingly in his forties, thickset, with a high forehead and large round curious eyes. A small trimmed black beard juts straight down from his lower lip like a hairy tongue. He smiles at Michele. The other cardinal is thin as a sword and older, with a perpetual sour scowl on his face. He has the habit of tapping his long index finger with its unclipped nail on the armrest. Both cardinals wear their four-pointed hats perched on the tops of their heads.

Cesari and Michele listen in silence while the two cardinals discuss in Latin the work that Cesari is delivering to the younger prelate. At the last moment, Cesari invited Michele along to the showing. 'You might as well come. Cardinal Del Monte always asks who the artist is and, if I say it is me, he knows I am lying.'

The sour-faced prelate, introduced as His Eminence Cardinal

Borromeo, gestures at the painting, as if to wave it away. 'Finally, Cesari, you deliver a piece on time. But a bowl of fruit and a vase of flowers? We need saints, martyrs, crucifixions, the Blessed Virgin, religious images to instruct the people in their faith. This looks like the work of a Protestant from the Low Countries, or worse, something a Frenchman might do. Keep in mind, these days the Holy Father is making life difficult for artists, as well as for prostitutes and especially sodomites. He forbids any painting that does not express the discipline of our faith. No more grotesqueries.'

Unexpectedly, the younger prelate, Cardinal Del Monte, speaks up. 'I must say, Your Eminence, my opinion in this case differs. The Holy Father has suggested we leave austerity to the Protestants, and more, that we counter that austerity with imagery, colour, ornament, a delightful celebration of our Christian life. Let us reaffirm the predominance of the Vatican and Rome.' Del Monte adds a few lines in Latin which the other cardinal understands but not the two artists. He continues, 'I believe this painting before us is the furthest thing from the grotesque. I have never seen such exquisite detail, as if from life. Miraculous. You see the window there in the painting, reflected in the glass of the vase and again on the surface of the water?'

'Yes, quite fine. But still ...'

'And the fruit. It appears real. I can almost smell it.'

Cardinal Borromeo shakes his head. 'It appears far too real. The peach has a spot of rot starting, and several gnats circle above the plums. The vine leaves are speckled with stains, and that pair of over-ripe figs have split open and are oozing a viscous liquid. We need per-fection, as a sign of Heaven. Fruit is the work of God; it must therefore be perfect.'

Michele steps forward, although Cesari puts his arm out to try to stop him from speaking. The younger artist ignores him. 'Your Emi-nence, God made the fruit but not all fruit is perfect, and all fruit rots eventually. God, it seems to me, also made the gnats.' The painter's stance indicates a natural aggressiveness, his stocky body, thick eyebrows, eyes black and penetrating, all speak of a sense of resolve approaching arrogance.

From the side, Cesari glances at Michele in silence, his mouth grim, wondering if this northerner will lose him the commission to paint the vault of the Contarelli chapel in the church of San Luigi dei Francesi, which he is hoping to start the next week. Cardinal Del Monte commissioned it several months before and Cesari has yet to begin work on it. Cesari, Michele has noticed, is skilled at gaining commissions here, there, and everywhere, but seldom finishes anything. He has too many projects going.

To Michele it seems that Cardinal Borromeo resembles a vulture dressed in scarlet robes. The older cardinal declares to Del Monte, 'It is up to you if you want to accept the painting. It has nothing to do with me. But I would suggest you only deal with artists who know how to hold their tongues. I plan to suggest to the Holy Father that we need a list of forbidden subjects, that is to say, prohibited images, for painting, just as we have now the highly effective Index of Forbidden Books. You might reflect on it. In any case, I must now take my leave. I have countless duties awaiting me. *Te salvere jubeo.*' He rises from his chair and departs, his long robes swishing with a subtle susurrus, hissing in distaste as he sweeps out the door.

Del Monte watches the door close, waits a moment seemingly deep in thought, and then turns to Cesari. 'Tell me. Who painted it? And don't lie to me, Cesari.'

Cesari, with a nod of his head, indicates in silence Michele standing next to him. 'I would gladly take credit for it, Your Eminence, in fact the subject was my idea, but I must be truthful. This young artist who works under me painted it, following my instructions.'

'It is marvellous. Life itself. What is your name? What else have you done?'

'I am Michelangelo Merisi from the village of Caravaggio near

Milan. I have done little but small heads, flowers, and fruit in the background of larger paintings since I came to work in his studio.' He indicates Cesari, who shrugs and nods. 'Nevertheless, I have been able to paint a few of my own works in what little spare time I have.'

'You have a tongue on you. His Eminence Cardinal Borromeo did not like what you said, or that you said anything at all, but I believe it is a sign of independence, a good indication in an artist. I believe I am an excellent judge of men and an even better judge of painters.'

'Indeed,' Cesari nods.

*Thinking only of his commission,* reasons Michele.

The cardinal turns to the older artist. 'Cesari, please begin the work I commissioned for the Contarelli vault. It is time. I have waited in patience for you to get started. We must have it ready for the Jubilee Year, for the arrival of Christian pilgrims in the city. What is the delay?'

'The Jubilee Year? 1600? That is still over four years away.' Cesari pauses, glances to the side, trying to come up with a good excuse for what Michele knows now is simply gross incompetence.

The cardinal explains, 'There is much to be done and all of it will take time. Hold your tongue. I do not want to know why you delay. But get started this week. I tire of your excuses.' He turns to the younger painter. 'Do you have any other works of your own? Anything with figures?'

'I have one other painting in my room. It is my only painting with a figure. A self-portrait.'

'Only a self-portrait? Why?'

'I cannot afford models.' Michele smiles, liking this cardinal. 'I myself am the cheapest model I can find.'

Cesari comments: 'I believe the painting will not be to your taste, Your Eminence. I find it dark, rather brooding. He was ill at the time that he painted it.'

*And you did nothing to help but dump me at the Consolation Hospital, where I had to earn my keep by doing quick paintings for the prior.*

The cardinal bristles, 'I alone will decide, Cesari, what I like and what I do not like.'

Cesari nods slightly, takes a half-step back and remains silent.

'What happened? What was your illness?' the cardinal asks Michele.

'It was not an illness, Your Eminence. I was injured. Kicked by a horse.' Michele decides not to mention that he actually grew up on a farm and feels profoundly stupid for not knowing better than to walk behind an animal.

Del Monte turns again to Cesari, 'Now, is this young artist contracted to you?'

Michele speaks before Cesari can reply. 'We have no term of contract, Your Eminence. I do piece-work, as required.'

'Good. Then, by God's grace, you will come to work for me. I want you to move into my palazzo and I will serve as your patron. I will provide a studio for you to work in and commissions for you to earn your bread and more. And as many models as you require.'

Cesari scoffs. 'But, Your Eminence, you have seen but one painting. Only one.'

Del Monte gazes at it again in silence. He does not speak for a few moments. The two artists wait. Michele watches the cardinal as he stares at the painting. Never taking his eyes from the canvas, the cardinal says, 'Yes, a single painting. But look at it. Like nothing I have ever seen before. With this one work, he obliterates all the Mannerists of our day. With a single peach, he makes the rest of the painters in this city look like amateurs.'

---

Crowds of gypsies, gamblers, and prostitutes mill under the towering columns in the portico of the Pantheon, built by the Romans but later turned into a church, Santa Maria dei Martiri. Moments after the presiding cleric of the church had left for the evening, hurrying across the piazza, the sordid throng started gathering in the portico. At the west end of the porch, now several card games are in play with the crowd around the gamblers placing bets on their favourites. Several cheats are at work as well. At the other end, young men roll dice against the wall, including the seminarian who was left behind to watch the church in the evening. Marked cards and loaded dice are as common here as lice in the hair of a beggar. The young gamblers blaspheme when they lose their games. Meanwhile, gypsies slide through the crowd looking for purses to lift, and prostitutes make eyes at men or tug the sleeves of possible clients. Eventually the city guards will arrive to move everyone along with a half-hearted insouciance, performing their duty in an atmosphere of weary lassitude at having to go through these motions again and again every night fully knowing that as soon as they quit the piazza and move on to other pressing tasks, such as a glass of wine at the local tavern, the crowd of gamblers and revellers will begin to drift back under the portico, necessitating the repetition of the same removal a number of times in a single evening. It is like trying over and over again to keep waves from drenching a sand-strewn strand.

Michele watches as a fetching gypsy girl, a lick of flame no more than fourteen, sidles up to a young fussily dressed aristocrat boy with a feather in his cap, takes his hand, strokes it sweetly, and begins reading his palm in order to tell his fortune. The boy is enamoured, taken with the girl, his eyes swimming with delight. So enticing is the strumpet, and so lost in his reverie is the boy at the touch of her hand, he closes his eyes and never notices that she has slipped his expensive ring off his finger. She finishes reading his palm and whispers his fortune close to his ear, breathing on his neck. The boy pants, looking faint with excitement. She steps back, smiles, and slides into the crowd. Michele decides not to intervene, figuring the wealthy boy will find it an even trade: his ring, one of several no doubt, in return for the momentary attentions of a sweet slut.

As Michele turns away, his attention is drawn to a face in the crowd. It is a face he cannot stop staring at. He never approaches the man but keeps in his memory for future reference the sharp contours of the man's cheekbones, his drooping sad eyes, the high forehead. But there is some indefinable quality about it. It is the face of a rapacious, feral animal, but it also reveals a disturbing timeless aspect, as if the man possesses tremendous patience and will, a kind of static, dangerous immobility behind the suppleness on the surface. The man seems keenly aware of everything and everyone around him, his eyes slowly taking in his surroundings as if he wants to swallow the world and all in it entirely. Michele will never forget that face. Never.

Soon after, as Michele is leaving the portico, he bumps into one Claudio Peretti, a wealthy patron who has commissioned a painting from him. They walk together for a while down a nearby street discussing when the patron can come view the work in progress. Then Peretti heads off on his own.

---

A few days later, Michele meets a young artist at a taverna and is so taken with the young man that he immediately hires him as his apprentice and model. The boy is thrilled. Michele decides to insist that if the cardinal wants him to move into the palazzo, then Mario, his new apprentice and model, will have to come as well. Will the cardinal agree? He is sure that Mario will like the arrangement—the boy appeared half-starved—but he has no inclination if the cardinal will. Mario told him that his parents are dead and he lives with his older brother. Michele senses that now is the time to insist with the cardinal, while Del Monte wants him. In fact, he suspects that Del Monte longs to be his patron more than he himself desires to live in the palazzo and have a studio and easy access to models. He feels his star is on the rise. And he knows that Del Monte senses this too. It is the time to strike.

Though living in the cardinal's palazzo will present its problems and restrictions, the streets will be his other home, where he can vent his frustrations. They will serve as his arena for swordplay and drinking, and the place to hunt for the faces of his various models. The thought of a model for his next painting has him excited about his plans with Mario, and he hurries toward home.

---

'You want what?' Cardinal Del Monte sits behind his desk, in momentary shock. In the study's fireplace, an olivewood fire sparks and fills the room with a pleasant scent.

'Yes, I would like the boy to have his own room and to share my studio. He will serve as my apprentice, grind pigments for me, and do other various jobs as required. I will need an apprentice in order to accomplish all that you will require of me. I cannot come to Palazzo Madama without him.'

'An apprentice? I suppose it is sometimes done.'

'Yes, Your Eminence. An apprentice and a helper. He will also serve as a model for a number of paintings I have planned.' Michele notices that the cardinal gives him a questioning look, as if he wonders if he is lying.

Del Monte drums his fingers on his desk for a few moments before answering. And then he makes his decision. 'This is most unusual, but my palazzo has sufficient rooms to fulfill your request. But have him move in several weeks after you. The way things are at the moment, with the Holy Father's views on licentiousness, I would not want anyone to raise any suspicions. Be careful, Michele, do not start unwholesome rumours.'

'I will keep what you have said in mind, Your Eminence. I hear the Pontiff has ordered that all windows and grates in convents in Rome be boarded up so no one can watch the young nuns as they dress and undress. Is it true? His main concern seems to be his entry into Heaven. I have seen the Holy Father processing through the city barefoot.'

'Do not question the Pope's orders against licentiousness or his pious activities. He is only thinking of the coming Jubilee Year when the city will be overwhelmed with visitors. He has urged the cardinals to spend whatever it takes to make Rome as splendid and glorious as possible. Through the embellishments of art, we must re-establish the Holy City as the heart of Christendom. But Clement himself knows little about art. He has asked a few cardinals, such as myself, to consult with him about how best to make Rome again the jewel of the Christian world. So, you, my son, will be kept very busy.'

# ❈ THE ASSASSIN ❈

On the portico of the Pantheon this evening, someone has been watching me. A young man with wiry black hair and a stub of a beard stares unabashedly. I fear he might approach me and try to strike up a conversation. I dislike people I don't know engaging me in talk, especially when I am working. Why is he interested? I despise being stared at. I am the one who looks.

And I *am* working. Apparently, a young nobleman named Claudio Peretti who likes slumming, enjoys coming here to play cards. Several months ago, this rich fool was involved in a duel out along the Appian Way. He was lucky that day. His blade sliced open the gut of his adversary while he himself went untouched. He managed to kill his enemy but his enemy has friends, in fact a brother who has enough wealth, and the right kind of connections, to hire me to exact revenge. My black-hearted accomplice, Enzo, cruises the far side of the portico, searching with me for the same man. The brother informed us: 'Look for a tall man with a white scar high on his neck under his left ear.' If he is here, we will find him and begin our routine: follow him home, see if he walks alone and takes any dark alleys, begin to plan our approach. We take our time, Enzo and me. There's no hurry. No reason to hurry. Patience is my greatest talent. Let him begin to relax after the killing of his enemy in the duel. Let him begin to trust that no one will seek revenge, that he is safe.

Without much trouble, Enzo and I find him. He has finished his card game just as the warning of the guards' approach goes up and the portico empties, like a bucket of dirty water swirling down a hole. It amazes me how rapidly the gamers and gamblers can snatch up their coins, slip away their cards, fold up their tables, and leave the

Pantheon's porch deserted. When our target leaves the portico, we follow at a short distance.

Immediately, another man joins Peretti. They are in no hurry but saunter along the street as if without a care in the world. We move closer without attracting attention. The street is crowded with those out for a stroll on this fine spring night. I realize that the other man is the one who was staring at me earlier in the portico, and a ripple of nerves runs through my belly. I don't know why but I sense some problem. Peretti enjoys speaking in a booming voice, a sign of his standing and his authority. We can hear him easily, although the other's voice comes to us in snatches.

From what I can make out, the other man is an artist and Peretti has commissioned a painting from him. They are discussing the arrangements and Peretti says that he wants to come to the artist's studio to view the work before it's finished. The other does not appear pleased with this arrangement. Peretti ignores his hesitation. The artist names a street in the Ortaccio quarter. 'Via Salummi?' Peretti asks, repeating what the artist has just told him. 'I know it. On next Wednesday, then, in the evening.' If the artist lives in the Ortaccio, I can understand why he does not want the wealthy patrician coming to his place. Like most artists, he likely lives in a sty, filthy and cramped. Maybe he keeps a whore there, or a wife with a clutch of brats underfoot.

Peretti and the artist part. Enzo and I leave off as well. We have what we need, and this street is much too busy to attempt anything at the moment. In any case, Peretti keeps turning and looking behind him. Luckily three boisterous, half-drunk youths have come from a side street and have been walking in front of us so we remain undetected. However, as the artist takes his leave from Peretti and strides down a side alley, he turns around at the last moment and, without my wishing it, our eyes meet. He stares, as if he recognizes me from the portico. He halts and continues his staring. I am uneasy. This could complicate our plans. Enzo and I hurry away. Ultimately, though, we are pleased, because we know that Via Salummi is a shadowy passageway like many in and around the Ortaccio.

---

The next Wednesday evening, after the nearby church tolls the evening bells, Enzo and I wait in an alley leading to Via Salummi. The darkness weighs silent and heavy. A steady rain fell earlier and now a drizzle continues, stippling the puddles in the street. We see Peretti approach alone and pass the alley and we fall in behind. No one is about as the rain has increased again. The rain's pounding masks the sound of our footsteps. The old women who constantly lean from

their windows to nose out what is going on in their street have been driven back by the downpour. The street turns and narrows. We creep along behind for a while and then put our plan into action. I hurry past Peretti whose shoulders are hunched against the rain. He glances up as I pass. I spin about and face him. 'Signor Peretti?'

'Yes? What is it?' He raises his head to confront me, a questioning, imperious look in his eyes. I think, *My face will be the last thing you see in this life.*

At that moment, Enzo runs at him from behind, sliding his glistening rapier into his back. Six inches of shining, blood-soaked sword comes poking out of the man's belly. He looks down at himself in shock. 'Vito Troppa sends his greetings,' I say as Peretti falls to the ground, his cape slipping from his shoulders. Enzo yanks his blade out. I roll Peretti over with my foot and stick him again in the throat, for good measure. Blood gushes from him in a stream and mixes with the rain.

As we begin to walk away, I turn and hurry back to remove his boots of fine leather to take with me. I pull them off and, standing to leave, I see on the wall a picture of Jesus staring at me as if he has been watching all along, and disapproves.

———————

A few days later I go alone, perhaps foolishly, to this artist's room on Via Salummi. Certain persistent thoughts continue to trouble me. *Did he recognize me? Did he know that Enzo and I were following Peretti?* I have asked around. His name is Michelangelo Merisi, a young painter on the make, from a village near Milan. His studio is not hard to find. I knock and shove my way in. Another man is there, tall, wide-shouldered, with a flame of red hair and a menacing look on his long, ugly face. The room is gloomy, with only a single lamp lit. In the back, a jumble of paintings, frames, a cluttered workbench but I cannot make out any details. The walls look coated in grease.

'Who are you?' the young artist asks. Before I can answer, he adds, 'Ah, I recognize you. You were at the portico the other night. And I have seen you before on Piazza Navona.'

Perhaps this is foolish, to confront him in this way, but I must know what he knows before deciding what to do next. Leave Rome immediately? Kill him? I ask him why he was staring at me in the portico.

'I am an artist. I study faces, and yours intrigues me. I would like you to be a model for one of my paintings.'

I pause. 'You pay?'

'Of course.'

'Then I can be your model. As long as you pay.' And in the silent pause, I cannot help myself. 'Did you hear about the murder of Signor Peretti in your street the other night?'

Red gives me an irritated look. 'What is it to you?'

'Close to home, yes?'

Merisi eyes me. 'Yes, it was. He was on his way here to look at a painting of mine he had commissioned. I lost a good sale.'

I am pleased to hear he seems more affected by losing a sale than by the man's death. If Merisi had been alone, I would have walked in and sliced him in half with my blade, but that is impossible now.

Red juts his chin out and bites his finger at me. 'A rotten smell has come to this room that was not here before you walked in.'

I resist going for my sword and remind myself. *I'm not here to look for trouble but to try to determine if trouble is looking for me.* 'No need to be insulting,' I counter weakly.

The young artist speaks up. 'It is no problem, Onorio. Does he not have an intriguing face? I will include him in a painting, I am sure of it. My painting of the calling of Matthew to Christ's circle. This fellow resembles a Jew, I think, though he wears no yellow cap.' He addresses me then. 'You know it is illegal not to wear your yellow cap.'

'Watch your tongue. I am no Jew.'

'Well, good for you,' Onorio says. 'But, let us leave this off. My young friend here is inclined to protect you for his own purposes, so I will go no further. Perhaps, when he is done painting that hideous face of yours, we will meet in the street and what will be will be. Your head on a plate, no doubt.' Red brushes me away. 'You can leave now. My friend and I have something important to discuss.'

I burn with anger but decide to leave. I will make this son of a whore pay for his tossed-off insults. I have my honour too, such as it is. I've killed better men than him.

I push out the door, slamming it hard behind me and walk down the cobbles of the street. When I pass the spot where we killed Peretti, I can see that a few bloodstains remain on the cobbles. At least Merisi didn't suspect that I had anything to do with it. I got what I wanted, and a gut-full of insults to boot. Too bad Enzo was not with me. The two of us would have ripped those *bastardi* apart. On top of everything else, he calls me a Jew. I should go back and slice him into pieces. I will wait and see.

The next night, I'm still angry at how they spoke to me. Sneaking down the alley near the artist's place, I come to his house and glance about. No one is in sight. I open the bag I brought and smear shit all over his door.

---

Vito Troppa, the man who hired me to murder Peretti, who killed Troppa's brother, paid me well. For the first time in a long time, I do not have to sleep in an alley with rats scurrying over my legs. I have my own room. A cell, really. Dank, cold, musty, yes, but a stone room with a pile of straw to sleep on. But money slips through my fingers like water. Perhaps I should say like cheap wine. I have not been sober in a week and, despite giving Enzo less than the half he expected, I will soon be penniless again. I do not like cheating Enzo but he will never know. Now that the warm weather is coming, I can pawn my heavy clothes and bedding with their maddening fleas and reclaim them early next winter, just like I do every year.

I find myself sober one evening, and already nearly penniless, I decide I must go out and mingle with the mob for that is the only place to find more work. I head out, cross Piazza Navona, which is quiet—a few Jews selling used clothing as usual—and on to Campo Marzio and the tennis courts.

Before reaching the courts, I stop to join a small crowd assembling to watch several charlatan Minorites, monks dressed in grey cassocks. One of the monks is passing his hands over the eyes of a blind man, urging him to open his eyes and see. Finally, the fake blind man opens his eyes wide and exclaims, '*Dio mio*! I can see! I can see!' This fellow, I am sure, has his vision cleared at least once a week on the streets of Rome. The other monk is collecting coins from the crowd, many of whom are taken in by this charade and would like their own afflictions cured. If I had one of those greasy grey cassocks, I myself would try my hand at this scheme but the robes are surprisingly difficult to come by. I leave the crowd behind and continue on my way.

Everyone who counts goes to the gaming courts. Three large courts of dry grass, surrounded by palazzos of the wealthy. A few go to play and others go to bet on those playing. Most go to strut about on the sidelines to the sounds of 'pock, pock, pock' and the shouted insults from both players and watchers. Some are there to catch the latest rumours, insult their enemies, and meet their friends. A few gatherings of men stand about, waiting their turn to play. Near them, others are down on their knees tossing coins for impromptu bets or throwing dice. Some search out whores because this is another favoured place where the prostitutes come to find customers. Fights break out with little provocation. Where money and betting are concerned, a small flame catches easily. As luck would have it, no sooner have I neared the courts than I am met by Merisi the painter. 'Ah, my Jew friend, still without his yellow cap!'

'Do not call me that,' I hiss. The red-haired pig does not accompany him tonight, but a boy, maybe sixteen, stands next to the artist, and a well-dressed older man, his forehead heavily lined, a feather in his velvet hat. The boy is pretty. A bit too pretty. Perhaps the artist is a sodomite and this is his special lamb.

'Who is your friend?' I ask. 'Your lover?'

'Don't be insulting. Mario is my apprentice. He will be a fine painter one day. Young, yes, but talented. Mario, meet one of the most interesting faces in all of Rome. I will paint him soon. I have a piece in mind, dealing with Saint Matthew, but must finish several other works before I can begin to capture this fascinating visage you see before you.' He turns to introduce the older fellow. 'And this is Prospero, who speaks well of me to all the established artists and among the gallery keepers.'

*The painter doesn't even ask my name. I truly am nothing more than a face to him.*

'He does look Jewish,' says Mario.

I shake my head and again resist pulling my sword. The painter's left hand is bandaged.

'What happened to your hand?' I ask as if interested.

'Nothing. Nothing important. A fight with a groom. A bastard who cannot hold his tongue. You agreed to be a model for me, yes? When I need you.'

'I said yes before, did I not?' I do not like these artist-types and their hangers-on. I wish the groom had taken him down. I add, 'I will not model in that squalid room of yours. It stinks.' As if I am not living in a filthy cell myself, but he is ignorant of that. I see the artist clutch at his rapier and then change his mind.

He says, 'Worry not. I will not be there much longer. I have been lucky enough to find myself a patron. I will be moving into Palazzo Madama shortly.'

I look up then and I see approaching from a distance a small crowd of young men, led by none other than Vito Troppa, swaggering and laughing like the drunk he is.

*Cazzo ... merda. . . .* I do not want to be seen by Vito. I turn my face away, trying to hide, but he struts right up to me and greets me like an old friend. 'Luca!' and gives me a half-drunken slam on the back. 'How are you?'

'*Bene,*' I mumble and feign disinterest in the hope he will leave. If Merisi discovers that Vito is the brother of the man killed by Peretti in a duel, the artist might start to draw lines, making connections to me. *Damn. What luck. He's an artist and likely very skilled at drawing lines.*

Troppa lingers. 'What have you been up to? Spent my money yet?' He is teetering drunk, but his friends, seeing several prostitutes ahead, have passed along. Before I can reply, he stumbles on to join them, without waiting for an answer. But the artist has heard and a confused look crosses his face. Before he can question me, I take my leave, and follow Troppa into the crowd.

## ⊷ THE ARTIST ⊷

Late afternoon on a sunny day, the sharp light pours through the narrow streets at an angle, throwing shadows across Piazza Navona; shadows of Jewish pedlars, noisy charlatans offering cures for this and that, the crowd hurrying along, a few stopping to purchase oranges or *ciambelle* cakes from wandering vendors. In the distance, four or five boys kick a rag ball around. A handful of police guards and several prostitutes linger at the margins, watching. Michele wanders along the outer perimeter of the long piazza, head down, his mind still sparking from the full day he has spent painting in his studio. The session went well, he was pleased with the results: the boy's head, the alluring look in the eyes, the skin, the mouth. Mario was his model and he proved to be excellent—patient as a lizard on a sun-drenched wall. For Michele, being immersed in painting for hour after hour is indescribable. Nothing is more appealing. His hands still tingle.

Michele halts his blind march and looks across the piazza. Ignoring the passersby and the pedlars near him, one of whom is singing lines from Dante's *Inferno*, he notices the shadow of a building on the ground. The shadow replicates the roof line and dome of the church of Sant'Agnese in Agone. He considers the way light and shadow touch. They caress each other in a kind of dance, the one drawing the other after as light recedes and shadow advances. He can barely breathe. The fierce beauty of the world stuns him. It is all achingly beautiful, even the rotting cabbage in the gutter, the cobbles speckled with bird shit and spittle. Riveted, he gazes dumbfounded across the piazza. A few of the Romans on the square notice this strange man who seems frozen in a paralysis of looking, the sole still point in a frenzy of activity.

Michele is too agitated to eat. He knows he will enjoy no sleep this night but will lie awake, the vivid, shining highlights of his day sparking in chaotic flashes before his eyes. His mind is raging with a vitality that seems inextinguishable. He needs action, a way to purge the intensity. He needs to swing his blade with abandon, to smash someone, to be crushed himself.

A young man approaches, attempting to walk around the artist, this madman in his path. Michele grasps the handle of his rapier in its sheath. 'You!' he shouts.

The young man recognizes the artist who is beginning to gain a reputation in Rome, both for his paintings and for his unpredictable belligerence. He manages to give the painter a wide berth and avoid a confrontation. Michele lets him pass. Bursting with uncontrollable energy, Michele dashes on with no destination in mind.

Several hours later, after he has stalked back and forth through the city in an attempt to tire himself out and burn through his passion, Michele enters a tavern, downs a pot of wine and rents the charms of an ordinary prostitute, a slim girl with curly black hair and bad skin. Back in his dwelling, he lies enfolded in her arms, like the crucified Christ in a scene of the pieta, his passion slain.

After the prostitute departs, Michele searches through the small trunk holding his precious books, some of which have been given to him recently by Cardinal Del Monte: Dante's *Divine Comedy* and a single antiquarian volume on colours and pigments. Also, an ancient, leather-bound Bible. And lastly, a manuscript copy of Leonardo da Vinci's *Codex Urbinas 1270* that Del Monte offered him as a gift soon after they had first met, telling him that it contained all he needed to know about painting.

When the Cardinal gave him Leonardo's codex, he told Michele: 'Take these words by the great Leonardo. Read them. But do not just read them—study them, memorize their rules, and follow those rules to the letter for he was the greatest of painters, a genius among artists.' It sounded like a well-rehearsed sermon from the cardinal. Though Michele had nodded in agreement, he was put off by hearing great praise for another artist, even Leonardo, whose Last Supper he had viewed and studied in Milan as an apprentice.

Michele wanted to reply by saying that, 'Yes, Leonardo was at times inspired, but ultimately he did so little painting, I believe he didn't truly enjoy it. He seemed more interested in designing siege engines and catapults.' But Michele didn't say that. Instead, he simply observed, half in jest, 'But he painted with his left hand.'

'That is of no importance,' the cardinal had responded with impatience.

After the cardinal had given him the codex, Michele returned to his room and put it aside. To this point, he had refused to open it. Maybe he would consider it if his own work and inspiration dried up, but that had not yet happened, not once.

Now, taking up the Bible, he pages through it, not reading as a religious man or cleric would but as an artist searching for inspiration.

The great epic stories that bookend the Bible hold no interest for him. *Genesis* and *Revelations* he considers too majestic, too grand and unimaginable; he cannot picture anything in his world that relates to them. He seeks, rather, the intimate, personal scenes: the crucifixion of Peter (even the crucifixion of Christ is too monumental, too momentous); the scenes of common people, Magdalen, Saint Matthew, and Saint Paul, these men and women of the East who had other real lives before becoming emblems and icons of history; the Holy Family like any ordinary family; Abraham and his son, Isaac; the horses and donkeys; the supper boards on trestles laid with meats and fruits, their smells somehow in their colours, both enticing and nauseating; the doubting apostle Thomas, so failingly human. He does not read deeply but pages through the testament at random, glancing here and there seeking ordinary scenes, exactly as he glances from side to side as he strolls through this great city of Rome with its ancient rubble and ruins scattered everywhere, its crumbled history, and its passionate present-day Romans leading tangible lives.

Putting the Bible down, he recalls his wanderings that afternoon and evening, what he saw with his own eyes: the endless display of humanity and life, a city throbbing with activity, with beauty and pain and suffering and anger and hatred and violence and love. He recalls the sleeve of a man's striped silk blouse, a pair of hands holding playing cards, the tattered leaf of a grape vine, a boy's wide mouth with creases at the corners, the way the skin wrinkled when an arm was bent, an old man's watery eyes of pale azure, a blue only seen after a cleansing storm, a three-legged dog running away. Eyebrows, cheeks, ears, hand gestures, the sheen of a knife, a look that passed from a desperate prostitute to a possible customer, the hem of an old priest's cassock swirling like black water as he shuffled, the way a coin fell sparkling through air, the way each droplet of water on a white chrysanthemum reflected the entire piazza. He knows with certainty that many of these images, or versions of them, will soon appear in his paintings.

––––––––––

Michele enjoys talking about painting with young Mario as they take breaks from their canvases, young Mario who is full of wide-eyed enthusiasm and eagerness to learn. Mario turns from his canvas one day and says, 'Might I ask a question? One thing I have noted is that you don't begin with thumbnail sketches that many artists use to work up an idea. It appears that you paint your sketches directly on the canvas.'

Michele tilts his head and gazes into the painting he stands before while he answers. 'I believe I must dive directly into the work

without delay. It is the only way to capture the drama and the dream of the moment.'

Though Mario is his apprentice, Michele does not play the domineering master in their relationship. He considers them friends. He likes Mario's questions. They make Michele reflect on what he is doing. In the act of painting, he becomes a mindless tempest, everything spilling out with a spontaneity and rush that overwhelms any logic or reason he can apply to his work. While painting, he is busy directing the storm and the swirling wind and trying to make it come to life on the canvas. In those moments, he has no time for reasoned thought, for deliberation. But afterwards, when a question like this comes from Mario, he enjoys contemplating why he works the way he does, why he paints the pictures he paints.

Mario adds, 'And you never seem to have any backgrounds in your paintings. No hills or fields or city buildings as in the work of other masters.'

Michele stares at the floor a moment and then looks up. 'Simply because Rome comes alive in its streets and piazzas, in its taverns and tennis courts. Everything of importance happens in the streets—

genuine life lives in the streets, on the surface of the city. In the same way, the surface of paintings is what matters to me. The background will clutter up the surface. That is why, in some cases, I attempt to have the image break through the frontal plane of the painting, to have an angel's wing, a foot, or a hand, seem to come out of the painting and into the world.'

Mario has an impish way about him at times. He believes that Michele will never be angry with him no matter what he says. Mario displays a wide grin. 'Those words you just said, did they come to your lips just now or have you given them careful consideration?'

Michele smiles. 'I do like your questions, Mario. But now I feel as if you are grilling me for possible entry into the Academy of Saint Luke, that assortment of Mannerist painters and other sycophants. Avoid them, Mario, avoid them. They will destroy your art.'

————————

That evening the two friends enter a tavern they like to frequent near Piazza Navona. The Gatto Bianco serves cheap wine and food and is therefore the haven of poor painters, apprentices, and young women on the make. It's also one of the few establishments in the area that commonly ignores the law that bars prostitutes from entering taverns. The owner, clearly, is a friend of the police so they tend to leave his inn alone. As the two friends enter, they see a pair of girls they know waiting in front of them. Annuccia, stocky as a little bear, only comes up to Michele's shoulder. She has long hair, red as the light of Mars, and when she's angry, her eyes could set one on fire. The other girl, Fillide, a brunette, taller, prettier, moves with a grace and elegance that belie her occupation. Her face can take on a haughty look that makes her appear higher class than she is. Both girls have recently moved to Rome from Siena. Michele has seen them around, working the streets, Fillide wearing a stomacher of fine serge. He likes these two girls but hears rumours that the regular Roman prostitutes around the piazza do not appreciate the newcomers crowding into their territory, nor Fillide showing off her success by wearing fancy clothing.

As the girls enter, a painter named Livio, a scoundrel who Michele feels receives far too much recognition for his shoddy work, announces in a loud, mocking voice, '*Ola*, Annuccia! Not a bad arse for a stump!' Not one to suffer fools gladly, Annuccia makes an obscene hand gesture, and spits back, 'You have a pretty terrific arse yourself, *cazzo*, or so the boys tell me!' Next to Livio, a half-drunken, slumping apprentice bellows, 'Ah, you're nothing but a whipped whore! Two Sienese whores with their noses and arses in the air.' Fillide sticks her tongue out at him. 'You two beggars are shitting yourselves with fear,' she says calmly, in a way that shows she is not the least bit rattled by their catcalls.

Three other local prostitutes at the back of the tavern stand up, stalk forward. Suddenly everyone in the crowded tavern is pushing and shoving, shouting slurs and insults. 'Who told you two cows to come here and move into our territory? Clear out or else,' one of the Roman prostitutes shouts. 'O, go ride a bull, you fat pig!' Annuccia screeches. Then she uses one of the most offensive insults to issue from a Roman mouth: 'You're a cop's slut!' Soon the tavern is mayhem, and Michele and Mario jump in. Michele plants his fist in Livio's face. One of the prostitutes tackles Mario, taking him down. Within moments, six constables rush through the door and collar a dozen people. They catch Michele in the sweep, along with Annuccia, Fillide, and Livio. As for Mario, he crawls on his hands and knees under several tables, slips out a back door, and escapes.

Those arrested spend the night in jail, in one large room, where the catcalls and slagging continue into the early hours, although the actual physical confrontations are over. Meanwhile, Mario has fled to Palazzo Madama where he breathlessly asks to see Cardinal Del Monte. Mario has no success getting past the guard until he convinces him that the cardinal will be interested in hearing what has happened to 'his painter'. Finally, the guard lets Mario in and hands him off to a servant who ushers him into the presence of the cardinal. Mario blurts out, 'I am Michele's apprentice. He's been arrested!'

'Settle down. Calm yourself. Tell me what happened.'

When Mario has finished recounting the event, the cardinal sends his major-domo to the jail with a note in his own hand ordering Michele's release.

The next morning, the artist stands before the cardinal, his head bowed, trying to hide several bruises on his face. Mario waits next to him. The cardinal shakes his head. 'Michele, it is time for you to move in. You are starting to gain a reputation on the streets. The fight with the groom, and now this ... I need you close by so I can keep an eye on you.'

'I did nothing.'

'Of course not.'

'I was in the wrong place at the wrong time.'

'But with your usual high temper?'

Michele shrugs. Mario decides he must speak. Standing as tall as he can, he takes a half step forward. 'Your Eminence, it was not his fault. The prostitutes, Annuccia and Fillide, were being ganged up on.'

The cardinal addresses Michele. 'These prostitutes, they are friends of yours?'

'Yes. One has agreed to be my model.'

'Ah, I see. Well, that complicates things.'

Mario, wide-eyed, exclaims, 'Why?'

The older artist holds him back, nods to him to be silent. 'We will move in today, if Your Eminence wishes it.'

'Yes, it is time. I will have my man show you and Mario your rooms, and you will share a large studio. Perhaps I can keep you a little more under control while you are dwelling in my house. You have no plans to allow these prostitutes also to move into my palazzo, do you?'

'No, of course not,' Michele replies. 'Although, forgive me for saying so, but I hear that the Vatican itself supports an army of prostitutes. In any case, do not worry, Your Eminence. I promise in future to be more discreet.'

'That should be a new experience for you.' The cardinal smiles, shakes his head, and eyes the painter. 'If you were not such a marvellous artist ...'

Michele raises his head and looks directly at the cardinal. 'Ah, but I am.'

'Yes, Providence has blessed you with great talent, Michele. And confidence as well. But not much humility.'

Michele has truly grown fond of the cardinal. He has such an avid, cultured mind, loves art and science, his face can grow florid with excitement at the appearance of a new painting or news of the discovery of some novel scientific apparatus. And he loves his meat and wine, keeps one of the richest tables among the Vatican clergy. Michele smiles. 'Your Eminence, the great Mantuan artist, Andrea Mantegna, once said, "An artist's talent has always helped a cardinal rise to the rank of pope."'

'You flatter me, Michele. But I have little interest in the Papacy.' Del Monte smiles back at the artist. 'Let me say this. Your artwork reminds me of the special purple ink long used by the popes—just like the ink, instead of fading with age, your paintings seem to grow brighter.'

'Thank you, Your Eminence, but I would prefer that its brilliance be appreciated right from the start.'

'Ah, my son, you must learn patience, and to submit to God's will, as must we all.'

———

Within several weeks, Michele and Mario have settled into their rooms, the latter arriving sometime later than Michele as agreed. They share a large studio with windows facing north. At opposite ends of

the studio, each sets up his own easel with a canvas mounted on it. On Mario's, several figures can be seen, looking out at the viewer. The canvas on Michele's easel is blank. He sits staring at it.

'As I'm sure you know, the name Michelangelo Merisi da Caravaggio is being heard all over Rome now,' Mario offers from a couch, where he lounges in a luxury he has never before experienced in his young life. 'For good and ill.'

Michele stands, moves to the window, and gazes out on a sunny, cool, spring morning, the sky clear over Rome, its streets busy with citizens going about their business. 'Yes, I am succeeding, to a certain extent, it's true. And, unfortunately, I have also gained something of a reputation for my anger. It is as if my creativity needs bursts of energy to flower.'

The nearby palazzos and squares are soaked and streaked in sunlight, the sprinkling of rain that came in the night evaporating from the cobbles. The moisture gives the world a charming sheen. He can see in the distance the high branches of umbrella pines dancing in the wind, sparkling with light.

Mario continues. 'Your reputation is mounting. All the young artists are taken with your new style, which is something they have never seen before. I am amazed. You already have your imitators, a sign of your influence.'

'Hmm.' Michele is pleased to hear this news, but the praise his work receives from all quarters is never enough. What he knows he needs now, in order to succeed as an artist in this city, is a large commission. Any artist of any repute would be asked to do paintings for church interiors. That is where genuine success lies, that is how the serious wealth flows down from the church to the flourishing artists of Rome. The patronage of Cardinal Del Monte is a good first step, but much more needs to be accomplished. 'Mario, do you recall that Jew who is not a Jew we met at the tennis courts?'

'Yes. I believe his name was Luca. What of him?'

'I'm thinking of using him as a model in a large painting I have planned. Also, do you remember? That other fellow came by and asked if he had spent his money yet? I learned later, that man was Vito Troppa whose brother was killed by Peretti in a duel. Peretti was one of my patrons. He was murdered in the street outside my old studio. Why do you think this Troppa gave money to Luca?'

'I have no idea. Is it important?'

'I don't know. But I wonder.'

---

The canvas before him remains blank. With the eyes of a stunned animal, Michele stares at it. He has an idea, the spark of an idea, for a first painting to produce for the Cardinal, but it has not yet burst into flame. Mario is out, the studio is quiet. Silent, muted light falls through the north-facing windows. Michele sits. The blank canvas shimmers.

On the worktable, consisting of boards laid on trestles, his brush of miniver lies inert, lifeless until he reaches out and picks it up. His brush-hand then comes alive, seems to float free of his body, flickers across the canvas like a dark moth, intoxicated, almost maddened, by the glow of the finely-woven flax canvas, the smell of pigments and oils. With his other hand, he brushes dark curls from his forehead. He sniffs through his wide, thick nose, runs the side of his hand through his moustache and tugs lightly on his short beard.

An intriguing thought comes to him. *Every painting comes out of nowhere, starts as the faintest, most distant star in the firmament of the imagination, and then takes colour, takes form, becomes existent in the world.* He licks the brush, dips it into pigment, and continues.

The next day, when Mario enters their studio, Michele stops painting and looks at him. 'Mario, just in time. Will you sit for me? I need you as a model for this piece. As you know, His Eminence is a great lover of music, so I have decided to paint some musicians for this first painting for him. Here, hold this mandolin.' Michele picks up the instrument from the table and hands it to his friend. Without a moment's hesitation, Mario nods and sits on the stool near the canvas. Michele adjusts Mario's hands on the mandolin, turns him slightly in his seat. '*Perfetto*.'

Over the next few weeks, Michele works tirelessly on painting the four musicians. Four androgynous youths from the waist up, one with his mostly bare back turned to the viewer, another on the far left plucking at a cluster of grapes, Mario holding the mandolin, and the face of Michele himself, at the back, staring straight out, his mouth half open, as if in ecstasy. They all have dark, arched eyebrows, thick black hair, translucent skin lit with the light of an Italian dusk.

When Michele is satisfied with the painting a few weeks later, he presents it to Cardinal Del Monte. As the cardinal's eyes rove over the work, Michele cannot help but hold his breath. Del Monte, in his clerical robes, gazes at the painting in silence, his look impossible to gauge. He places his hand on his chin, his index finger over his lips. He grunts but Michele is unsure if he does so in disgust or pleasure. He is terrified that the cardinal will object to the painting's obvious licence, will insist on having it destroyed and that Michele be thrown from the Palazzo Madama back into the streets, or worse, have him arrested. Del Monte turns to him, smiles, and says softly, 'It is marvellous.'

Michele breathes out and relaxes. '*Grazie*, Your Eminence.'

The cardinal continues. 'Of course, I cannot allow it to be seen by my more conservative colleagues. But I will surely be displaying it for other friends, those who can appreciate what the finest painting can accomplish. No one else in this city is doing work of this magnificence. Where did you gain such skill? Have you studied the Old Masters?'

His chest swelling with appreciation for his patron, Michele says, 'Truthfully, Your Eminence, I believe that Nature is my teacher, not the Old Masters. I want to see the world for myself, not through their eyes. And this city of Rome is a wonderful stage. The streets and squares offer me a never-ending theatrical display.'

'Well done, Michele, well done.'

'Your Eminence, there is something I must ask of you.' Once again, Michele feels that the time is ripe for further requests.

'Yes, what is it?'

He proceeds to explain in detail his needs for his next painting, a major project. He has received a large commission from a church in the city, with the help of the cardinal himself. When Michele finishes his explanation, the Cardinal complains, with a smile: 'I provide you with a fine studio in my palace, well-lit from the north as you requested, and I myself gain an important commission for you and now you want more. A second studio, in my cellar storerooms, in which to work? On top of that, you request a small barrel of good olive oil from my kitchens. Are you planning to replace my cooks, my pastry chef? And a good quality, sizable mirror? And how many models did you say? Seven? It never ends with you. One request after another.'

Michele replies, an ingratiating smile softening his words. 'Your

Eminence, I do believe you could spare several of your two hundred servants to clean out the room in the cellar and provide me a little space in which to work. Our regular studio, while I appreciate it greatly, does not provide the correct quality of light, the dim atmosphere, that this particular painting requires. As for the olive oil, I need it to soak the paper I place over the windows. It is necessary to give the light a kind of opalescence.'

Cardinal Del Monte soon relents and allows Michele the use of the space. The painting that Michele recently delivered to his patron, his first major work, *The Musicians*, has convinced the cardinal that his young artist is a painter of incomparable skill and talent. 'He paints miracles, and not always the religious sort,' he later tells several of his colleagues in the Vatican.

---

In the early spring, Michele is arrested again. This time the police guards stop him while he is walking by himself between Piazza Navona and Piazza Madama, shortly after the midnight bells. The police have seen that he is wearing a sword. Michele is surprised, because the law against wearing rapiers in the street is seldom enforced. He recognizes the constables from the brawl in the tavern. The two guards harass him and search his person. The one with the scar under his eye pushes him up against a wall, while the other, a massive bear of a man with the drained eyes of a dullard, stands close by.

'Empty your pockets.'

'Why?'

'I said empty your pockets.'

Michele frowns and shakes his head in disbelief but proceeds to pull from a wide pocket in his doublet a metal tool with several long thin sharp points. The constable holds it up and stares at it.

'What kind of weapon is this? I have never seen one like it.'

'It is not a weapon but a new apparatus used by artists like myself. It is called a compass.'

'Looks like a weapon to me. You are under arrest. Come along.'

'You *cazzo*, you cannot do that.' Michele considers running, or hitting the constable in the side of the head, but the other burly guard gives him second thoughts. He also wonders what Del Monte will think about him being arrested a second time and he decides not to make things worse. 'The compass, the tool, belongs to my patron, Cardinal Del Monte.'

The constable looks up quickly at the name of the well-known cardinal but continues anyway. 'It is no tool, but a weapon, a kind of fancy dagger. Come with me, now.'

Michele decides not to resist, suspecting that as soon as the captain in charge hears the cardinal's name, he will be released.

Back at the jail, he waits in a plain dim room without a table. A Captain of the Capitoline police enters, holding the compass forth in his palm. Michele is immediately put off by his wide florid face, his thick lips.

'Where did you get this?'

'It belongs to my patron, Cardinal Del Monte. The compass, as it is called, is a device that modern painters use for measurement. And as a painter for the cardinal, I am allowed to wear a rapier as I go about my business and the business of the cardinal. I receive an allowance from the cardinal and I live in his palazzo.'

'I see.' He pauses, weighing the compass still in his hand. 'Since you are a member of the cardinal's household, I will release you. You will no longer carry this weapon about the streets but will leave it in the cardinal's workrooms.'

Michele pictures himself snatching the compass from the constable's hand and driving the sharp point into the man's eye. He rises to leave and the captain hands him the compass.

'It is not a weapon,' Michele mumbles, and stalks out the door.

---

On the cardinal's return to the city after travelling north with the Pope, Del Monte is informed of the arrest by his major-domo, Lorenzo. The servant, glaringly jealous of the young artist's friendship with the cardinal, has taken it upon himself to know everything about the painter who has so disturbed the tranquility of Palazzo Madama.

Lorenzo has been in the cardinal's service for seven years and, through skill and subterfuge, has risen to the top post among Del Monte's staff. The cardinal trusts him and expects to be informed by Lorenzo of all affairs that have to do with his palazzo, his staff, or his artists. Lorenzo makes it clear from the first day of Michele's appearance that he disapproves of the painter from the north. He does not hesitate to suggest to the cardinal that allowing a foolish, intemperate artist to take up residence in Palazzo Madama is a mistake. Michele senses Lorenzo's dislike. The major-domo always insists on greeting Michele with an arrogant smirk.

Lorenzo reports to the cardinal that he has followed Michele to his courtesan's house and discovered that the woman is a witch who has laid in stocks of small skulls, hair, fingernails, human skin, the navels of infant children, the eyes and teeth of dead men. He claims to have seen her slinking to a local graveyard at night to collect clothing from the dead and rotten flesh which she takes back to feed later to her lover. The cardinal takes all of this news with a grain of salt.

After hearing a report about the arrest from Lorenzo, the cardinal later calls Michele into his antechamber for a discussion. Michele explains that it was a misunderstanding about a compass, that the Capitoline guards had no idea what the tool was meant for and had considered it to be a weapon.

'And you were able to refrain from stabbing anyone with it?'

'Your Eminence, I was tempted, I must say, to attack the Police Captain, to punish him for his stupidity. And now that I know that your man, Lorenzo, has reported on my doings in your absence and disparaged my honour, I cannot say what I might do to him in thanks. He is an exaggerator and a liar.'

'You seem half angel and half fallen angel, Michele. A marvellous painter, if a bit rebellious. But you harbour a devil inside, one you should exorcise with haste. Beware your darker nature.' He pauses. 'And leave my major-domo out of this. He is only considering my needs.'

Michele nods and, for once, holds his tongue.

'On another subject, while I was travelling these past few days, one of my fellow cardinals said he wished to discuss your paintings with me. He claims you obtain the effects in your works through devilry, through witchcraft. This belief, I trust, holds no relationship to the truth?'

'Of course not. I employ a brush, pigments, and a fine eye. Occasionally, I have recourse to a mirror to reflect the sun or a lantern to cast a strong light, but these are no less tools than a brush.'

'Consider yourself warned. This particular cardinal—I will not reveal his name—supports a faction of Mannerist artists who denounce you in public. They go about the city deploring your art. I believe that this is a personal attack on me as well, as I am your patron, but I do not respond to such remarks. You, however, are known to draw your weapon at the least slight. Resist. As I said, beware your darker nature. Do not be drawn into quarrels.'

## ⚜ THE ASSASSIN ⚜

The thought will not leave me, day or night. Does the artist know? Has he connected me to the murder of Peretti? Peretti's friends are asking around, to try to determine if anyone knows more about the murder. Even certain acquaintances of mine have been approached. Vito Troppa told me even he has been approached. It feels like there are hounds on the scent, seeking me out. I must go to see Merisi again. I must, or I will never get this out of my head. Or am I panicking? No, I must. It is a foolish thing to do but it might also save my head. Where was it he said? Palazzo Madama? He's coming up in the world, this young scoundrel.

A few hours later, at the weary end of afternoon, I wait outside the palazzo. After a while, I see him enter the street. I am not stalking him this time. Merely want to talk. I step out from the shadows.

When the painter sees me, he asks, 'Why is it I never see you selling used clothing in the square like the other Jews?'

*Again, he calls me a Jew. Just because he wants me to model as Matthew, or Levi the tax collector. I guess Matthew was a Jew in the old stories. It seems I will be more real to him as a figure in his painting than I am in real life. But I will hold my tongue. It's information about the search for Peretti's murderers I seek.*

I try to keep my voice steady as I speak, without showing my fear, or my anger. I must be patient to get what I need. 'You are lucky, my young friend, that, unlike you, I do not burst into flames at the least slight. I understand it is your custom. Fighting every night of the week.'

'What is it to you?'

'Just a comment.' Merisi turns to go and I say, 'Mind if I walk along?'

'Why would you want to do that?'

'I am interested to see how a young artist like you so easily finds trouble.'

Merisi starts walking and, without turning his head or looking at me, mumbles, 'Do as you wish.'

How can I broach the subject, I wonder, without raising suspicion? I try to think of something to say but nothing comes. I cannot talk to him of art for I know nothing of those skills. I know how to slit throats and drive a sword through a man's guts, but that is no subject I wish to discuss. The silence eats at me as we walk along together. I decide I can do nothing but come right out with it, foolish as that may be. As we saunter along, I say in as casual a manner as I can muster, 'Have they found Peretti's killers yet?'

'Killers?' He stops and stares at me. 'Why do you say "killers"? Was there more than a single murderer? And, if so, how do you know this?'

'There often is, in such cases,' I say weakly, knowing I have misjudged. I change the subject. 'Where is your beastly, red-haired friend tonight, the one who was at your studio when I came by?'

'Onorio? He's exchanged his rapier for a heavier sword. He has decided to go north and fight for the French. Whereas I still have my slim, sharp blade right here.' He taps the handle of his weapon. 'With it I can penetrate the toughest cloth.' He sticks his finger into my worn doublet.

'You did not wish to accompany him?'

'No. I am here to paint and I have a responsibility to my patron to do so.'

We stride along in silence for a few dozen paces. As we near Piazza Navona, the narrow street we are walking along empties out into the spacious square. The artist halts again. He looks into the piazza, but I cannot see what he seeks. I suspect he is not looking at anything out there but his own thoughts. He turns and confronts me. 'Did you kill Peretti?'

Uncontrollably, I stumble backwards. 'Of course not!'

'If you did kill him, I will see your head mounted on the Ponte Sant'Angelo, despite my interest in painting you. Peretti was a strong patron of my work, who had promised to keep buying my paintings, and he's been snatched away. Now go away and leave me alone. I am joining friends and I do not want them to know that I associate with someone like you.'

Glad to have a reason to escape, I slink off, realizing that I must kill him before he goes to the authorities.

Later, when my anger has abated, I reconsider. I cannot kill him immediately. Patience is my supreme talent. I must wait. People have seen me with him. His friend, Mario, for one, and others. I must wait long enough for his friends to forget that I know him. Then I will strike. Like a viper one never sees lurking in the grass.

As I head back to my hovel, I meet an occasional acquaintance, a ragged man, his face covered in scabs, who I know is a thief. He looks me up and down with a ridiculous, superior grin. This look tells me without his saying a word that he knows something I do not.

'Well, what is it?' I ask

'Your friend, Enzo. He's been arrested.'

'For what?'

He shrugs, runs his hand through his lanky, dirty hair. 'You would know better than me.'

'What are you suggesting?'

'Suggesting? I'm not "suggesting" anything. I say it out loud.'

He hurries off, and I head for a tavern where the kind of information I seek can be found.

_____

The tavern, in the Monti district, is one of the seediest in Rome, filled with lowlifes like me. An acquaintance who frequents the place—I can hardly call him a friend—will provide the information I need. For a price. Everyone calls him Carlo the Ear.

I enter and through the fug and smoke, I glance around. There he is, sitting in a corner, alone, tall and straight and dark and looking dreadfully drunk. I know from previous encounters that the drunker he gets, the straighter and taller he sits. I squeeze between tables and a chaos of disarranged stools and benches to reach him. The noise in the place is deafening and frenzied, the smell of unwashed bodies and cheap spilled wine gagging me, though I have a strong stomach for such things. I approach. 'Carlo. Can we talk? I need information.' He tries to sober up, focuses his gaze on me. The thought of a scudo or two coming his way straightens him out. At the next table, two drunks are playing the _morra_ hand-game to see who will buy the next round. I'm glad to see they are ignoring us.

'What information?' he asks, staring up at me. I take a seat across the table from him.

'Enzo Rondini has been arrested. I want to know what crime the authorities have charged him with.'

Leaning forward to ensure our conversation remains private, he says, 'Knowing Rondini, it could be for any number of crimes. You know that as well as I do.'

'Yes, but one crime caught their attention. Which is it?'

Carlo taps his long index finger, with its knotted knuckles, hard on the damp wooden table.

Fumbling for two coins from my purse, I place them before him. He taps again, I place another _baiocchi_, and he nods. I wonder if

I have been too hurried in my actions, revealing my desperation for this news.

'He murdered a gentleman.'

My breath catches. The room, though filled with raucous laughter and shouting, goes silent to my ears.

'When? When did this happen?'

'Over a year ago. His accomplice at the time, who recently confessed under torture, has fingered him.'

I breathe out and relax a little.

Carlo leans forward and eyes me, his bushy eyebrows rising. 'Why do you want to know?'

'That is of no importance.'

'No one pays good coin for information of no importance.'

I decide I must flee, before Carlo, with his penetrating mind that gathers information from all quarters and spreads it to the world for a price, learns why I want to know about Enzo. At the same time, I am wondering if Enzo under torture will confess to our most recent murder and drag me to the executioner with him.

Carlo grins, showing his gums, waiting for my answer.

'The trouble with you, Carlo, is that you are willing to sell information to anyone, anyone at all.'

'That is my job, is it not? I have sold information to you, information you appeared eager to have. Why so desperate, my friend?'

'Not your business, Carlo.' I begin to rise from my seat.

Conciliatory, he says, 'Join me for a pot of wine. I will buy.'

'No. Generous of you to offer, but I have an appointment to attend to.' I can see in his eyes that he knows I am lying.

———

The next day, on a warm spring evening, I head over to the tennis courts. I hope to see the painter, to begin to learn his patterns of behaviour, his habits, where he goes and when, who he goes with.

When I was young, I used to hunt small birds with stones. Nothing has changed in my life. This is the same.

As I arrive at the tennis courts where a good crowd is gathering, the painter spies me and shouts in my direction, 'Ah, the Jew who is not a Jew. Come here.' It is an order filled with arrogance. He waves me over. He stands with his young friend, and several other young men. Dandies, fancy silk-dressed artists, people who believe they are better than me, with their noses in the air.

I approach, with nonchalance, trying to show that I am not at his beck and call. 'Do not call me that. I have told you before—I am no Jew.'

'I am sorry if I offend. It is a joke of mine. Do not take it personally.'

'What is it you want? Why did you hail me?'

'I have news.'

Suddenly I feel as if I stand on air. 'What news?'

'Tomorrow morning I begin that important painting. The one I mentioned to you before, in which you will play the role of Matthew, the tax collector. Are you ready to model for it?'

I pause to consider. I need the money. If I can get a few scudi from him before I slit his throat, so much the better. He takes my hesitation in the wrong way.

'I will pay well. Or rather, my patron, the Cardinal, will pay well.'

Still I hesitate. 'How long will it take?'

'I have no idea, but I would need your services for at least six months, until next autumn, let us say. I am known for painting quickly, but this is a major work. Each day you must be available at a moment's notice.'

I nod. 'When will you pay?'

'I will pay you at the end of each day's sitting, if I am happy with your ability to remain posed. You can hold still for long periods?'

I want to say that as a murderer and assassin I am skilled at waiting, holding my breath, not stirring for hours and hours at a time. My patience, my lack of passion, has proven most helpful to my work. I smile to myself and want to say out loud to this fop that I practise my own particular form of art: the Art of Murder. Instead I say, 'I am capable, I am sure, of holding my position for as long as needed. Nothing could be simpler.'

---

The next day I arrive at Palazzo Madama early. A servant takes me across the courtyard, through a door and we descend together to the vaulted cellar. *What is this?* I wonder. As I enter a large dim room, the artist is standing, holding out a costly silk doublet to a young boy. A small crowd of other models stand about the room, waiting. Merisi turns and greets me.

'Come here,' he says, leading me over to a table spread with a selection of odd-looking garments. 'Put this on.' He hands me a black velvet cloak and a floppy hat of the same material. All the other models in the room begin dressing. I count six others besides me. The artist gives one of the boys a feathered hat.

Eventually we are fitted out in the garments he wants us to wear. We stand in a line as he inspects us, adjusting a collar here, a sleeve there.

At the far end of the room, a massive canvas is resting on several easels. He leads all of us to a table that sits beneath a window. I watch as he pours a pitcher of olive oil onto a sheet of paper over a pan. Immediately his assistant places the oiled paper over the window. The window admits little light because the glass is now covered, but a mirror situated at an angle beside another window is casting bright sunlight and causing a contrast of deep shadows across the room.

He arranges us around the table, tells each model where and how to sit. Meanwhile, he positions two of the models a few feet away from the table, standing. He steps back and stares at the tableau, biting his lower lip. He strides across the room, turns around, and watches us as he adjusts the mirror. Then, moving around the table, he tells each of us, one by one, precisely how to position ourselves. Most of us at the table are told to stare at the other two models standing nearby.

He comes to me and adjusts the tilt of my head. The boy with his back to the canvas is ordered to spread his legs wider, the other boy to change the position of his right hand. Merisi places a few coins, several small cloth bags, and a book on the table. At first, the book is closed. He steps back and stares. Moves forward and opens the book. Steps back again, then scolds one of the boys, 'You shifted! Do not move! Move again and I will replace you. Do you understand?' The boy stares down, frowns, and nods.

The artist takes half the morning adjusting the stance and the hands of those seated at the table and the two models standing near us. One is pointing. At me. And I am pointing at myself as if to say, 'Me, you are calling me?' The artist steps back, watches, eyes us as if he is hunting small birds in the bushes. He subtly adjusts my pointing hand, as if I now point as much at the old fellow next to me as myself, as if to ask 'You mean him? You are calling him?'

The artist warns us. 'You must remember your place, your position, the placement of your hands and legs, the gaze of your eyes. Every day that you are here, each of you will take this precise position.' Then he retreats behind his canvas and starts to work.

After several hours, I ache with the stillness and cannot imagine how I will be able to stand this for an entire day when I feel such pain after a single morning. I was wrong about my training as an assassin serving me well for this work. Finally, he tells us to relax. His young friend Mario brings a basket of bread and cheese and olives, a bit of wine, to another table and we eat in silence. We models do not know each other. Do not care to know each other. We are all here for our payment and can think of nothing but how painful it will be this afternoon when we are back in place.

We finish eating and drag ourselves to the table with the book and coins and take our places. He remembers every detail. Slightly lowers and bends the tip of the pointing finger of Christ. The two young boys need numerous touches to regain their positions. He fixes my hat, just so.

We wait and he sits down across from us, near his canvas. I stare at the Christ model. I can also see the artist. He does not pick up a brush this time, just watches. For what seems like an entire hour, he remains utterly still. The look of concentration on his face is astonishing. I realize that, when it comes to his art, he has as much patience as me. At last, he walks around the table, leans over and lifts my arm the width of a coin, returns to his place. After another interminable wait, he rises again. This time he presses down the thumb on the hand I am using to point. Not all the way down. Part way.

He returns to his seat, leaps up, and shouts, 'You!'

We have no idea who he is yelling at. I still point at myself or my neighbour or somewhere between us, afraid to move. *Me,* I'm wondering, *is he shouting at me?* He is a tyrant and though I could slit his throat without a moment's hesitation, I have to admit that his arrogant, ferocious nature has me shocked and cowed, for an instant only.

'That is it, Luca. That is the look I want on your face. That look of confusion. Feel that look on your face, in your skin, fix it in your mind. Each time you sit in that chair I want that look on your face, those alarmed, questioning eyes, that slack mouth. Understand?'

I nod.

'You have such an utterly fascinating face, Luca. Astonishing.'

Thus, the first day passes and, at the end, we models flee with our coins in hand, ready to burst, to fly, to run, to wave our hands and arms about, anything to escape that cellar with its stillness and pain. I plan to spend the entire evening gulping wine to forget the long day and to forget also that tomorrow I will be back to do it again. Why? Because he handed out more coins than I ever

expected. I don't know if he himself is the generous one or if this generosity flows from the Cardinal, his patron, and I care not. Though I still look forward to slitting his throat, I will have to delay killing him until this fountain of coins runs dry.

## ⊰ THE ARTIST ⊱

*I have been working on the Calling of Matthew painting for several months now and that face, Luca's face, continues to fascinate me. I stared into it for several hours today, trying to get my painting of Matthew just right. Those wide-open, round eyes that always look a touch startled, that weak mouth, that high forehead that reveals the shape of his skull. The nose thin and straight, the medium-length bushy beard, the straggly hair. Again, there is something about those eyes—slightly aghast, as if he has seen things no man should ever see, and deep within them, a touch of horror. There are certain sights that scar a man forever, images that can never be removed from his eyes, scenes that have been burned into his vision. I sense he has witnessed acts that are beyond belief, beyond imagining. Such a face.*

Michele is about to start work again on his painting in the cardinal's cellar. He glances at his Matthew model, Luca, looks away, then goes back and stares at him.

'Luca, you seem to have arrived this morning in a state of high emotion. The look on your face is disconcerting. I see pain. Deep sorrow. Melancholy. You look disturbed. But there is a hardness too. This is not the face of questioning and confusion that I have ordered you to provide.'

Michele waits, watches him. *He appears incapable of listening to me this morning. His mind is elsewhere. The others are getting restless.*

He tosses his brush aside. 'You are all dismissed. You will receive no payment for today. Come back tomorrow and we will try again.'

---

Michele stalks into his studio in the Palazzo Madama, ignores Mario standing at an easel, and drops into a chair.

Mario watches as Michele slams his fist down on the table and groans. 'You have returned early,' notes Mario, who pauses before a painting of Saint Jerome, holding his brush up, its tip bulbed with scarlet pigment. He wonders if he should say anything more, in light of the mood Michele is displaying. 'I did not expect to see you until late in the afternoon.'

'Yes, my idiot tax collector ruined an entire day of work.'

'You mean Luca?'

'Yes. The same. The man is useless. He has the perfect face for my needs and he usually displays the exact expression I require, but today, his look was all wrong and he could not follow my commands.'

Mario turns to apply a brushstroke of scarlet to his painting but continues to listen, glancing back over his shoulder. 'Perhaps you should look for a replacement.'

'That could prove difficult. The painting is too far along to replace him. I fear I am stuck with him until the end.' His mood beginning to soften, Michele shrugs. 'What can I do?' Being around Mario always tends to calm his bad humour.

'Yes, I cannot imagine, after working on it for so long, that you would want to start over.'

'And, on top of that, one of the boys acts like he has a swarm of reptiles living in his trousers. He cannot stay still.'

'I was pleased you did not ask me to pose for this painting. I cannot hold a pose for five minutes.'

'No, no, Mario, you are much better than that. You did very well for me as a model on *The Musicians*.'

Mario asks, 'Why, this time, did you decide to have your models pose together? With *The Musicians* you had each of us pose separately and then unified the whole at the end.'

Michele considers this for a moment. 'I have been alternating my approach. With my first important painting for the Cardinal, I was worried that he would balk at the expense of models. I did not want to test his pocketbook. But now, I see that he appreciates and supports my work and the cost of models, however many and for however long I require them, means nothing to him. So, for this work I have the models posing together. I must say, Del Monte has been generous.'

'Yes, I hear he goes about the city praising you to the heavens.'

'So, now I see there are expectations put upon me. I must continue to produce works at the highest level, and quickly. Thus, the tax collector delays me for a day and makes me want to murder him.'

---

Entering Piazza Navona in the late afternoon, the shadows stretching their legs, Michele is greeted by his wealthy friend, Prospero, who is just exiting the square. *The feather in his velvet hat,* Michele thinks, *his signature.*

'Have you heard?' Prospero, placing his hand on Michele's forearm, asks, wide-eyed.

'Heard what?'

Prospero is hesitant, unsure how he should proceed. 'A note … about you … on the statue of Pasquino.'

Michele knows that the ancient Greek statue known as the Pasquino, on a street just off the Piazza Navona, is used as a place for Romans to post anonymous messages at night, berating their enemies, political leaders, or even the Pope, for various activities that the authors find reprehensible. Sometimes these messages are light-hearted but as often as not they air bitter grievances or outbursts of jealousy. The statue of Pasquino long ago lost its arms, signifying the ultimate efficacy of these posted diatribes.

'A note about me? What does it say?'

Prospero shakes his head and looks at the ground. 'I would rather not be considered the messenger of ill tidings. You had best have a look yourself.'

With a sinking stomach, Michele hurries across the piazza and down a street a short way to the constricted Piazza di Pasquino where the statue is located. *Why do I care what they think of me? Fools and half-wits. Jealous hacks.* He sees the ancient, worn, and broken statue before him. A half-dozen men stand about reading the various notes stuck to the statue's stone base. Michele approaches and searches for the one pertaining to him. He finds it and reads the diatribe written in a poorly composed poetic form:

*As for the artist Michelangelo Merisi*
*a foreigner from the north*
*with a ridiculous accent like stones in his mouth*
*the darling of cardinals*
*the keeper of young sodomites*
*he is terribly overrated*
*no talent there at all*
*no understanding of art*
*no understanding of the great masters of the past*
*a painter whose paints are mud*
*whose brushes are sticks*
*whose models are whores and thieves*
*why do the young artists of Rome like to imitate him?*
*This is like floundering ducks*
*seeing their reflections in scummy water.*

Ripping the note off the statue, Michele stuffs it in his pocket and turns away. He stalks across Piazza di Pasquino, turns and walks the enclosed square again. *Who could it be? Who would write such insulting lies about me?* He knows he has enemies among a certain class of artist in the city, those who envy him his artistic skill and his luck in gaining the support of well-off patrons. Some of the younger artists have started to imitate his work, inspired by his novel approaches to painting. The older, established artists, he realizes, are most likely his enemies, those he competes with for the support of patrons and for church commissions. *Could it be Cesari? Probably not. Too busy, he wouldn't bother.* Another name, however, keeps coming back to him—Livio. Recently Livio accosted Mario in the street and asked him why it was, when they were arrested for the fight in the Gatto Bianco, that Michele spent only a single night in jail while he, Livio, and the others spent a week there. He went on to complain that Michele is accorded special treatment by the Capitoline guards. In ending his conversation with Mario, Livio had said, *Someone should bring Michele down.*

———————

Cardinal Del Monte sends a servant to bring the painter to his study. Michele follows the servant through several anterooms. The servant knocks and enters, Michele in his wake. A late morning sun streams through the high windows of the study, illuminating a forlorn painting of Saint Francis on the wall, a skull on the saint's table.

'Michele, I hope I am not disturbing your work.' The Cardinal turns to glance out the window. 'It is a lovely day, is it not?'

'Your Eminence, I hope you have not summoned me to discuss the weather.'

The Cardinal smiles. 'You have a way of saying what is exactly on your mind, no matter the consequence or who sits across from you. I both admire this attitude and find it troublesome. However, you cannot offend me. You are an artist and I only expect the unexpected from artists. No, I believe this manner will only be troublesome for *you*, in the end. I suggest you make some effort to not be put off by people, to not respond with a viper tongue.'

Michele pauses and considers this suggestion. 'You are correct, Your Eminence. Still, I am who I am and I remain hopeful that you have not summoned me to discuss the weather.'

Del Monte grins and shakes his head. 'We will leave the weather to itself. I have heard that you are working on a large painting in the room I have provided you in my cellar. For the commission I arranged. Yes?'

'It is not a lie.'

'I see. Might I come and view this painting later today?'

'With all due respect, Your Eminence, no, you may not.'

Del Monte again shakes his large head. 'You surprise me endlessly, Michele. Why might I not view a painting which is being done in my own palazzo, by an artist of whom I am the patron?'

'Please, Your Eminence, do not misunderstand me. I prefer no one to see my paintings until I have finished them. It is my way of working. I urge you not to insist.' He hesitates but then adds, 'I must point out, as well, Your Eminence, that the last time a patron wished to view one of my paintings before it was completed, he was murdered in the street outside my studio.'

'I trust you had no hand in the villainy.'

'I did not. What fool of an artist would murder his own patron? It would show a severe lack of common sense.'

'Seldom, my son, do artists and common sense go hand in hand.'

Michele nods and grins in tacit agreement. He shrugs his shoulders as if to add, *What can I say? You are correct, of course.*

'I understand,' the Cardinal concludes. 'I will not insist. But I do insist that you join me for dinner this evening. I have invited several colleagues interested in discussing your art. Will it be possible?'

'Of course. I look forward to it,' Michele lies with a smile.

Although Michele never enjoys these feasts hosted by the cardinal, he recognizes they are a necessary chore, a requirement to gain the kind of commissions he desires. He will be asked endless questions about his family background, his techniques, his ideas about art, and his opinion of other artists, dead and alive. He attempts to be pleasant at these proceedings but it always proves a struggle. The variety of meat and fish served is startling. Beef and lamb, of course; but also, delicacies Michele has never tasted before in his life: turtle doves, lampreys, crane, cormorant, sea turtle, and once, a gamey-tasting swan followed by a disgusting, oily peacock displayed with its feathers replaced after cooking. And rich wines from as far away as Sicily, as well as oranges, sweet lemons, pomegranates, nut cakes, hearts of marzipan, and rose liqueur. If anyone was being honoured at the feast, as sometimes happened—a new cardinal appointment, for example—the servers would be sure to bring out platters of fish heads decorated with carnations and sprigs of rosemary as a sign of homage. But, Michele notes, despite the high standing of the attendees, they still wipe their fingers on the tablecloths like any lowlife in a tavern.

## ⇥ THE ASSASSIN ⇤

The artist has asked me to join him and his friends this evening. I believe it is in celebration of the painter's birthday. He asked all the models for *The Calling* to meet him and his acquaintances at a tavern in the Campo Marzio. I am surprised as I'm told he does not like large gatherings. Campo Marzio is the seamy quarter where many of the poorer artists live and work, paintings and sculptures poking out the doors and windows of their studios. It is not a world I can begin to understand. And yet, I can see that much of the work there washes in on a tide of greed and lust for fame.

These artists believe they are better than everyone else, simply because they can mix pigments, slop them on canvas, and hammer a piece of marble into the face of a saint. I too have hammered faces, with my fists, but they were real faces and I was paid more for my work than these artists see in a year. So, who is better? I do not like going to the Campo Marzio quarter with all its airs and its uppity snobs, but the painter has been increasingly friendly and generous to me lately, so I have decided it would be wise to attend, to keep those coins flowing.

It appears that poor Enzo Rondini was no Judas and did not give me up for the murder of Peretti. I still recall seeing Rondini's head on the Ponte Sant'Angelo clear as morning light. I remember that day, young boys were diving nude into the Tiber. Their freedom seemed so refreshing and in such contrast to Enzo's state. Merisi's suspicions have faded. I believe he is pleased with my ability to hold my place while he paints. After the first few days of pain, I have done well. I am much better at it than the others, except for one old man who has been working as an artist's model for years. If Merisi only knew where I had gained my talent. On the other hand, he's such a scoundrel himself that perhaps he might admire me for my other, more criminal skills.

Amazingly, I am developing a taste for painting. His painting only. As we finished yesterday and I stood with the others at the door to the cellar waiting as he fished around in his purse for coins to pay us for a good day's work, I stared at his canvas. It remains unfinished, of course, but I was once again astounded by the look of it. I am not a man who knows anything about beauty, I have a hard time caring whether I choose a lovely whore or an old wrinkled crone, but there was something about this painting that caught me, that catches me still, I know not what it is, but the image comes to me in my dreams. Christ Jesus is pointing at me, calling me. In the painting, my eyes are wide with anticipation and confusion and questioning.

As I waited for my coin, I stared into my own face as if I were the artist, standing in his place, looking at me. It was a strange feeling, as if I were gaining a glimpse at how others see me and feel about me. Merisi has shown me something about myself I have never seen before, never knew existed. I am human. *Dio mio*, I am a human being. I never understood that. I thought I was simply an animal that went about disguised in a human face. But something else is happening to me. I am being 'called'. To what, I don't know....

I arrive at the tavern for the party and he beckons to me as I enter. 'Luca,' he says, waving me over to the long table where he sits, the centre of attention among his friends and the other models. He seldom calls me Luca. It is always 'Jew' or 'Jew who is not a Jew' or simply 'you'. I sit down on the bench with the group of models at the far end of the table. The artist is at the centre, on the other side, down from me. Everyone is conversing and grabbing for attention and Merisi smiles and laughs. Young Mario is seated next to him, and that fop, Prospero, sits across from him. Two whores are at the table as well. They are unknown to me but the painter spends a lot of time with the taller one. Not at the palazzo, of course. The cardinal cannot be seen to harbour prostitutes. It is bad enough to have several artists living there, who may or may not be sodomites.

Merisi looks happy, ebullient, his face glowing and flushed. The painting is going well, his reputation on the rise, and now his friends are buying him cups of wine. Several baskets heaped with oysters, mussels, and whelks circulate about the table and those who partake use their daggers to pluck the meat from the shells. We models are not saying much, a little out of our element. So, we drink and eat and watch. It gives me the opportunity to stare at his face, as he has stared at mine while I sat modelling for his so-called 'great work'.

His dark hair is long and curly, just covering his ears, slightly unruly and tumbling over the upper part of his forehead. It's a style popular among the young artists of Rome, as if he wants to pretend that he is still a member of the poorest of artists in this city. This is, of course, a convenient lie. He is no longer poor. One can tell because he wears a black velvet doublet with slits to show its silk lining, a clean white shirt underneath with wide, floppy collar. His cardinal patron is dressing him well. A down-curved moustache rests above his lip, accentuating a slight snarl in the set of his mouth.

I note that his dancing eyes reveal his enthusiasm, though his mouth looks sad. His eyes are watering, testament to the four empty terracotta jugs of wine in front of him. He moves his head as one person after another around the table toasts the occasion. The narrow beard down the centre of his chin leads this head-turn as he thrusts it forward in the direction of whoever is addressing him. With this simple gesture, he reveals his arrogance.

———————

The next day, he asks me to model as Saint Peter for another painting. He is planning ahead, he says, the next three or four paintings worked up in his imagination. Why not use me as the model for all the apostles? I wonder. They are all Jews, after all, and he believes I look the part. And why not use me to model as the Roman soldiers too? After all, I *am* Roman. I could be the soldier who thrust the spear into Christ's side. And I am the apostle Thomas as well. Like him, I am a great doubter. My Thomas would not push a finger into Christ's wound but would thrust his entire arm in up to his elbow, gripping Christ's heart and tugging it out. I know, I know, Christ in my little daydream is Merisi. Then what would I do with the heart? It beats still. I cannot put it back. What is done is done.

He is nearly finished with *The Calling*. I hear it will be installed in the Contarelli Chapel in the church of San Luigi dei Francesi, just in time for the Jubilee Year. I know nothing about art but, to my eye, it doesn't resemble a religious painting at all. Why would it? His models are street people, dressed up to look like what they are not. His canvas is a bit of theatre, a scene from a play. There's something wildly dramatic about it, the way the light stands out from the dark. Strangely, the dark parts brighten the light. On the other hand, the light makes the darkness darker and deeper. As if he has given us a view into his soul.

At his birthday dinner, I heard one of his friends use an unfamiliar term in reference to his work. I didn't know the word. Later, I asked him. 'What is this style you work in? What do you call it?'

He said, 'It is called chiaroscuro—a mixing of light and dark. Like life, yes?'

'Yes, like life and death.'

Finally, he is gaining his much longed for church commissions. The new painting he mentioned to me is a crucifixion, not of Christ but of Saint Peter. Who in the devil's name does a painting of the crucifixion of Peter? It will be one of a pair. The other is the conversion of Saint Paul. He has a younger model for that one. He told me the pair of paintings will go into a side chapel in the Church of Santa Maria del Popolo over by Pincio Hill near the Porta Flaminia. He believes I care, will be impressed, but it means nothing to me. It is no more than coin that I can live on. Imagine me playing Saint Peter and taking up permanent residence in a church. Me, a murderer and assassin. This is a strange city in a strange world.

A month after mentioning the new painting, the artist sends a servant to fetch me. I had no idea he knew where I lived. And now the painter is growing used to having servants to do his bidding. Before, he would have come himself, knocked on the door, seen the squalor I live in, smelled the rotting fish guts in the alley, but no, now he sends one of the servants the cardinal allows him to order about. He is a fake, this damned Merisi, likes to lie with whores and flash his rapier when it pleases him, and yet is the companion of cardinals. But I see him, I see right through him. He is no different than me.

I follow the servant, not to the cellar but to Merisi's spacious studio on an upper floor in Palazzo Madama. Three other models are there. A huge wooden cross on the floor. For a moment, I wonder if we will truly crucify someone, and then I recall it is me who is to be crucified.

'Luca.' He beckons. 'Come here.' He holds a pair of scissors. I stand in front of him as he studies my face. He starts trimming my beard, clipping my hair. He finishes and steps back. *'Si, si, bene.'* Walking to a table, he says over his shoulder, 'Get undressed and put this on.' He lifts up a white loincloth and tosses it to me.

On the spot, I shudder out of my clothes. I am not ashamed of my nakedness. I like my scraggy, bony body, with its several scars. Once I have got the loincloth cinched, he approaches me with a pot. Taking a handful of ash, he starts rubbing it in my hair and beard. I imagine I look thirty years older. They are all theatre, his paintings, all fake and show, but something about them intrigues me.

'Over here,' he orders. He tells one of the other models, who are already dressed in their rags, to lift the bottom end of the cross and Merisi himself lies down on it at an angle, his head lower than his feet, one limb out along the arm of the cross. 'I want you to lie like this,' he tells me. 'Just like this.' I have a strange urge to take the hammer nearby on the floor and drive a spike into his head but I resist.

He stands and I lie down, trying to take his place. It is a difficult position. The blood rushes to my head. I know I will be earning my money with pain and suffering again. He takes up a spike and touches it to my palm. I can see he would like to make the crucifixion of Peter as real as possible. But then he puts the spike on the floor and begins adjusting the other models, showing them how to crouch or stand, what to hold onto. Facing away from me, one of the models grasps a rope that trails along his back as he tries to raise the cross into a standing position. My feet are in the air, my head pointing down. Luckily, Merisi gives me plenty of breaks this time as my position is exceedingly uncomfortable.

I cannot imagine the cardinal liking the painting much, or his friends, or the church that has commissioned this maniac to paint it. But what do I know?

The next day I come back to his studio to pose again. The artist greets me at the door. 'You can go home. I have decided to use an older model for Peter.' The bastard gives me a coin for my trouble and dismisses me.

# ⊰ THE ARTIST ⊱

---

The look on Mario's face is all wide-eyed enthusiasm and excitement. 'Tell me. What did His Eminence say?' Mario rushes up to Michele, who is just entering their shared studio.

Michele stares at the floor in a failed attempt to hide his feelings. He raises his gaze to Mario and bursts into a wide smile. 'He said "yes". He agreed. We leave in a week.'

'I cannot believe it.' Mario paces aimlessly around the room, moving from window to window. 'I cannot believe it.' He halts. 'What else did he say?'

'At the first, he hesitated. He asked why I did not send a messenger with my request to the monastery and have the man return with the required pigments. But I explained that I must view the colours personally beforehand, to ensure I receive the best of the best, the highest quality pigments available. And I told him that with such rich, brilliant colours, I will be able to create paintings that the world has never seen, paintings to bring great honour to his name. This explanation seemed to please him.'

'Will we go alone?'

'No, no, not alone. It would be too dangerous. The roads north of Rome are thick with bandits and thieves. His Eminence will provide three of his guards to travel with us, and you and I will have the use of two fine horses from his stables.'

'And he will pay for all of it?'

'Yes. Everything will be provided. We will stop at inns along the way and His Eminence will also give me a letter to present to the head of the monastery to introduce us and ensure we are treated with the respect and cordiality expected for a party sent by a cardinal. He has given me free rein to purchase whatever pigments I choose, even providing me with Florentine florins instead of Roman scudi.'

Mario grins. 'This is a good day, a very good day.'

---

Almost two weeks later, Michele and Mario reach the walls of Florence shortly before the gates are barred for the night. Riding in under the Florentine flags with their red fleur-de-lis on a white background, they notice that the air stinks of sheep. They soon find the monastery of the Ingesuati order, locate the abbot, and present the letter from Cardinal Del Monte. The abbot is impressed.

'We are about to commence dinner,' he says to Michele and Mario. 'You must join us as our honoured guests.'

After their simple meal, Abbot Severino sits across from Michele and Mario at a table in the refectory, a pot of wine and three cups before them. The abbot pushes back the hood of his cowl. Behind and above him, a fresco of the Last Supper, poorly executed, fits uneasily into a trio of pointed niches high on the wall. Michele considers that the abbot's face reveals an alarming similarity to the Judas in the painting above but he sweeps the thought from his mind. He likes this friendly abbot, past middle age but not yet old, who appears less corpulent than the abbots of Rome, though at the moment his chin is shiny with grease. The other monks, hooded heads bowed, brown robes eddying, left the refectory after dinner to say Vespers, the prayers offered at dusk. The abbot and the two travellers are alone.

Michele drinks. Putting down his cup, he asks, 'A question, my good abbot. Why does the air here stink of sheep? It is a foul, oppressive smell, one we do not experience in Rome.'

'Ah.' The abbot nods. 'Along with silk and banking, wool is the primary industry of this city of Florence. From all over Italy, the Florentines gather sheep, and they export the wool throughout Europe.'

'I see. I didn't realize that wool was so important here. Is your order involved in the trade or do you trade in pigments alone?'

'You must understand, my son,' the abbot explains, 'we of the Ingesuati order no longer have quite the industrious monastery we had a century ago. We were famous then. No trade in wool, though. At that time, the entirety of Christendom would come to Florence to order our stained-glass windows, considered the most beautiful in the world. However, we no longer engage in any stained-glass work. However, we are still known for the quality of our pigments. Tomorrow morning, I will take you to visit the small workshops in the surrounding area where our monks produce those pigments.'

Abbot Severino reaches for his cup of wine and takes a gulp, a crucifix on a cord around his neck. He refills their glasses followed by his own, settles back, and relaxes. His is the only chair in the room with a back. The rest of the seats are long wooden benches. 'In my time here, I have gained much experience with pigments and colours: where to find them, how to make them, what they are and what they represent. I learned all I know from our previous abbot. Our monks are fine craftsmen, the best in the world. It is my belief that pigments are the blood and skin of a painting but they include more than that. For me, each colour is a living spirit and it is the pigment that gives rise to that spirit.'

Mario nods. 'As a painter, I must admit I have a much more down to earth view of pigment.'

'Ah, but let me add that I have realized that the change from simple, raw mineral to pigment suggests much more. If a black mineral, for example, can be brought through fire and be reborn as scarlet pigment, then any kind of change is possible in this world: evil can be redeemed, body can become spirit, the divine can come down to earth and be human. This is sacred magic.'

Michele remains silent but he begins to suspect that the abbot, and perhaps the entire monastery, are under the heretical spell of alchemy.

'And let me add,' the abbot continues, 'that colour both *reveals* and *conceals* the world.' He pauses and finally wipes the grease from his chin with the sleeve of his robe. 'It also reveals and yet conceals the heart of the artist.' He pauses and drinks. 'But enough philosophy.'

---

The next morning, Michele and Mario take breakfast in silence with the rows of hooded monks in the crowded refectory, a simple meal of bread, dried figs, and water. While they eat, a monk in the corner of the room, standing at a lectern, reads prayers from a large tome. Following the meal, the two visitors follow the abbot, in his voluminous robes and deep cowl, into the quiet garden cloister, bordered by a series of small ogival arches at each side. Walking across the cloister, the priest stops at the garden's far end and mumbles a quick paternoster at the shrine of San Giovanni, patron saint of the city of Florence and of pigments. He then leads them through a doorway and out into the street and the cool fresh light of a May morning. They walk past the Church of San Giovanni Battista della Calza and soon come to a row of low buildings that house the monastery's pigment workshops. The first hut, belching smoke at this early hour, stinks of sulfur. Michele and Mario slap their hands over nose and mouth, while the abbot inhales the foetid stench. 'Ah, Brother Cosimo is preparing orpiment this morning,' he announces and beckons them to follow him inside.

Abbot Severino turns around to address Michele as they enter the smoky, low-ceilinged room. 'We make the richest yellow orpiment available anywhere—sulfur yellow with a mother-of-pearl sheen.'

'I know it as king's yellow,' Michele says and the abbot nods.

Mario observes, hand still over nose. 'It stinks in here.'

'Yes, the stench of sulfur and arsenic. But only when it is heated. Once cooled, it will smell like garlic. We find the orpiment crystals in clays and marls near hot springs. Also, it is sometimes found on the slopes of volcanos. An important orpiment bed is located near Naples.' The abbot turns. 'Brother Cosimo, how fare you this fine morning?'

A tall, stooped monk nods his head. A cloth is wrapped tightly across his mouth and nostrils, and his right eye appears filled with clouds. He motions them over to a pot on the flame and they look in.

'What is the process?' Michele asks.

The monk speaks through the cloth. 'First we grind the orpiment crystals with a muller-stone until fine.' He takes a bowl and begins grinding with a crunching sound until the crystals turn to powder. He dumps the powder into a clean bowl and mixes it with liquid from several bottles on a shelf.

'What are those liquids?' Michele asks.

'The best white wine, not too much, and urine from a young boy. This we place on the flame, add crystal powder and boil until it thickens. You see, it turns a fine colour, like a sunset. When it cools, I will pour it into small glass bottles and cork it. It can be used immediately.'

Michele notes to himself, *eight bottles.* They then move along.

The next workshop doesn't stink so badly.

'In this hut,' the abbot explains, 'we make vermilion, which you might know as cinnabar.'

'I know it, yes, of course,' Michele says.

'Ah, but I doubt that you know our cinnabar. You have never seen a fiery scarlet like this. Most Italian painters use cinnabar found on the slopes of Monte Amiata right here in Tuscany.'

'Yes, that is the pigment I have used in my own work.'

'Our cinnabar comes from the Spanish town of Almaden in the province of La Mancha. The best in the world. It has no match for the fineness of its colour. It is terribly expensive, but I am sure the cardinal has the means to satisfy your needs.' He turns. 'Brother Giulio, explain the process for our guests here from Rome, friends of Cardinal Del Monte.'

This monk is no taller than a ten-year-old child and he wears a filthy cowl. His voice comes out high and piping. 'The making of cinnabar is a procedure of extreme complexity. We begin with the marriage of sulfur and quicksilver in the nuptial chamber of the retort. At first, the two planets, the Sun and Mercury, do battle but eventually they conjoin and give birth to a new being.'

The language he employs makes Michele wonder again if perhaps these monks are alchemists rather than brothers in Christ.

Brother Giulio continues, 'Five parts quicksilver to one part molten sulfur produces a black substance we call "the Moor". This is pulverized and heated in a clay retort and the precipitate is scraped from the clay walls. We then grind this with water for a long time, then dry it and grind it again and again. It is a slow process but we have prayers to say while we work. After much grinding—the more the better—this black substance magically turns scarlet. When the colour appears, it is like drawing blood from a dragon, or like a child being born. I keep one vial I have ground every day for almost ten years. Its colour continues to deepen.'

'Might I purchase that vial?' Michele asks.

'My apologies. No, that one is not for sale. But we have other fine cinnabars that you may purchase. You will be most pleased with them.'

They visit the other workshops that day, each employing at least one monk busily creating pigments from sources around the world. At the door of the workshop where ultramarine, or lapis lazuli, is being processed, two well-built young monks stand guard. The abbot explains, 'lapis lazuli, it's worth more than gold. It comes all the way from the Hindu Kush, through Persia. We obtain the raw material from Venice and here produce the rarest of rare colours.'

When they finish their tour, Michele makes his purchases, handing over the florins he received from the cardinal. He loads dozens of cork-stoppered vials safely into a heavy leather sack. Then he requests that the three guards who rode with them from Rome make their bed that night outside his door in the convent as protection against thieves.

Before they take to their beds, Mario says, 'You spent a fortune on these pigments. Do you really believe they will help so much in your painting?'

'With these pigments added to my skill as an artist, I will truly become the greatest painter in the history of the world.'

'That is quite the boast.'

'My young friend, it is not a boast, it is a fact. A great painter must demand the very best pigments in the world, and now I have them. Just watch over the coming months what I can do with them.'

Mario pauses, then says, 'I was fascinated with what the monk said about cinnabar. That the making of it can give birth to a new being.'

'Yes. Intriguing. As if the dark and the light can conjoin to make something new.'

The next morning, early, they leave for Rome.


## ⊰ THE ASSASSIN ⊱

---

I follow three old Jews pushing their rickety carts as they leave Piazza Navona and enter an alley to the east. The carts are stacked with clothing that a beggar wouldn't wear. No silk robes with ermine collars here, but I'm desperate. I haven't eaten in two days except for the moldy piece of bread and a rind of melon I found in a garbage heap. Even then, I had to beat off a long-muzzled mongrel to get at the heel of bread first. I followed that same mangy dog halfway across the city, knowing he would be able to smell out food that I couldn't see. And it worked. But my stomach is ringing like a church bell at a requiem. I could sell my sword but it's so nicked and worn, what would I get for it?

No jobs have come my way for weeks. The artist has disappeared. I have not seen him anywhere. The coins I received from him are all gone. A thief like me relies on opportunity, but no opportunity has presented itself. None. I can feel my navel touching my backbone. These Jew street merchants travel in packs for protection but, at some point, I hope that one of them will have to split off from the others and head to his own hovel down an empty street. Then I'll make my move.

I follow, not too close but keeping them in sight. We pass a butcher's shop, reeking of stale blood and I almost faint from the smell and my hunger. For once, my plan works. One of the three, his ill-fitting shoes flopping, bids good evening to the other two and pushes his cart into a side alley. I pick up my pace and hurry to the narrow street's entrance. He's halfway along it, and my luck holds—the alley is empty. Dusk is well along in this narrow passage. I pull my sword and run up behind him. He hears me and turns, a stiletto in his hand but before he can lunge at me, I hold the point of my rapier under his chin. His paltry weapon is no match for my sword and he knows it. He drops the stiletto onto the cart.

'Your money. Now.'

He sighs and reaches into the deep pocket of his baggy pants. The handful of coins he pulls out is pitiful. 'Is that all?'

'Too many sellers, not enough buyers.'

Snatching the coins from his palm, I turn and run.

---

Two days later, I stand outside the Palazzo Madama, hoping to catch a glimpse of the artist and plead my case for work, but he never appears. Towards evening I see a servant I recognize, the major-domo, Lorenzo, who exits the gates of the palazzo. I approach him. 'Where is Del Monte's artist? He seems to have disappeared.'

Lorenzo stares at me as if he does not recognize me at first. Then it dawns on him. 'Ah, you are one of his models. I recognize you. Yes, Merisi has gone to Florence.'

'Why?'

'I hear it is to purchase special pigments for his work. He is expected to return in a week or so. Why are you interested?'

'A man must eat. I seek work from him.'

'You would do well to find other employment. I do not believe that the cardinal's favourite will be around much longer.' The way he says 'favourite' with sarcasm and disgust, signals to me that the man is no friend of the artist's.

'You have a problem with Merisi?'

He doesn't answer, but asks, 'What is your name?'

'I am called Luca.'

'You seem to me to be a man of the world, Luca. Are you a man of the world?'

'If you mean by that, am I a man who knows how to help himself to what he wants, then yes, I am a man of the world.'

'Good. A criminal and a thief, as I thought. There's an obvious desperation written in your face. Walk with me and I will reveal what I know.'

Intrigued, I begin to walk in step with him and we lean our heads together in private conversation.

'This Merisi has been given an outrageous amount of money to purchase pigments in Florence. I know. The cardinal asked me to hand several sacks of florins over to the scoundrel myself. I don't believe the artist even thanked His Eminence. He takes it as his due. More coin than I have seen in all my years serving in this palazzo.'

'And so? What is your point?'

'If you are willing to work with me, when the artist returns, we can get our hands on the most valuable of those pigments with relative ease. Lapis lazuli, for example, which I heard him tell the cardinal he is planning to purchase. I can get word to you when Merisi is out. I will let you into his studio, you can find the stones, and then sell them, perhaps to another artist. Afterwards, you will give me half the money.'

'It sounds too simple.'

'When someone has more than he deserves, and gains it with such ease, he tends to let down his guard. Believe me, nothing would give me greater joy than to fleece this fool artist.'

'Why not do it yourself then? Why do you need me?'

Lorenzo sighs and is silent a moment while two soldiers walk past us. 'My distrust and hatred of the man are clear to everyone, especially the cardinal. It was not wise of me to be so forthcoming but it is not in my nature to hide my feelings. If the valuable pigments go missing, my room will be one of the first searched. I need a third party to handle this affair. I do it as much for the treasure it will bring as for the opportunity to humble this arrogant artist. Do you not find him arrogant?'

'Yes, I agree. I too find him arrogant. I will do whatever is necessary.' We continue walking along the alley. Like many alleys in Rome it reeks of shit and piss and rotting meat and cooking garlic drifting out of doorways. The air is heavy with the stench. It fits my mood. I know that if Merisi returns while I search his studio, I will have to kill him on the spot. I have done such things before, of course. But something— what it is, I don't know—gives me pause this time. I shake the disturbing thought from my mind. I know I cannot allow a single moment of hesitation if it comes to that.

The servant turns to head back to the palazzo. 'Let us work together then and make ourselves rich while we humble this bastard artist. Come see me in a week, in the early evening. He should be back by then.'

---

I keep myself alive that week by thieving a few goods here and there, and stealing food. For once, I don't have to compete with the dogs but it's a struggle. A week later, I'm waiting at the gates of the palazzo as the evening church bells toll. Lorenzo sidles out and glances back in before greeting me. Again, we walk.

'The artist has returned. I have discovered that tonight he and his friend will be heading out to a tavern. I do not believe either of them will be back until tomorrow. Saturday nights he likes to spend with his whore, and Mario goes with him. I suppose he has his own girl somewhere.'

'How should we proceed then?'

'I will come down to the gate at the tolling of ten bells this evening. You wait for me but stay hidden in the shadows. When you see me, follow me into the palazzo.'

'What about the guard at the gate?'

'Do not fret about the guard. I will take care of him.'

I don't know if he means that he will pay the guard for his silence, or simply make sure he is absent at the right moment.

Lorenzo continues. 'I will lead you to his studio. You will have plenty of time to search for the pigments. Look for the rich blue stones, in particular. That is the lapis lazuli. I will wait at the bottom of the stairs. When you find the stones, return to me and I will let you out.'

'You know that if he returns while I am there, I will be forced to kill him.'

'Do not worry. He is a fool who believes he is blessed and that no evil can come upon him. It will work. Go to see the artist Donetti on Piazza Santa Maria in Trastevere. He will purchase the stones and any other pigments you can collect. He is a man who hates Merisi as I do, so once word is out that the cardinal's artist has been robbed, this artist will keep his mouth shut. But do not take anything less than eight ducats per ounce for the lapis lazuli.' He turns and disappears back into the palazzo, hurrying up the wide staircase, taking the steps by twos.

At the appointed time that evening, I wait, hidden in the shadows, and he comes with a lit lamp in each hand. I enter and we hasten to the artist's studio. Lorenzo hands me one of the lamps, closes the door quietly behind him, and disappears. I begin my search. No blue stones on

the work tables. Or anywhere else for that matter. I see a few vials of pigment here and there but nothing that appears to be of value.

I spot something that flashes in my eye. I nearly fall over from shock but realize it is nothing more than a mirror leaning up in a corner of the room, beside it a pair of angel wings on the floor. I go over to the mirror, my lamp doubled and pulsing. I glimpse my ghostly face behind the lamp. Will this mirror remember my presence here, I wonder? Could Merisi call in a witch to investigate the depths of the mirror and discover what it knows? I curb these foolish speculations and continue my work.

I search without success, until I hear the bells of midnight. Finally, Lorenzo sticks his head in and asks, '*Dio mio*, what is taking so long? Have you fallen asleep?'

'I can't find them. I cannot find anything,' I hiss.

'What?'

'There are no valuable stones here. No pigments worth taking. I have looked everywhere. Places only a rat could squeeze into but nothing nothing nothing.'

'Idiot. Come with me. You must leave now before a new guard takes over for the rest of the night.'

I exit the palazzo and later wrack my brain trying to imagine where the stones could be. Perhaps he gave them to the cardinal to keep them safe. But Lorenzo would know about that, would he not? Perhaps he has hidden them in the house of his courtesan. Or somewhere else. One thing I do know, they are not in his studio.

# ⊰ THE ARTIST ⊱

---

Michele and Mario continue to live comfortably in Cardinal Del Monte's Palazzo Madama. They are no longer master and apprentice but the closest of friends. They paint together, eat and drink together, talk about art with each other. The older artist spends much time commiserating with Mario over the latter's lack of success, and tries to help him improve his work, by suggesting different colour schemes and loaning him certain models for his paintings.

Meanwhile, Michele has been assigned several servants of his own by the cardinal, and his reputation as a painter has further blossomed across the city. Numerous young painters are now imitating his realistic style. Works of incomparable skill and beauty continue to pour out of Michele's studio in the palazzo, and his income increases accordingly.

But Michele remains dissatisfied. He hears of other Roman painters who receive commissions from various cardinals, especially from Cardinal Pietro Aldobrandini, the nephew of the Pope, as well as from the Pope himself. These other painters talk of receiving outlandish sums and gold chains in thanks from the Cardinal Nephew. One day, Michele asks Del Monte, 'Why is it that I am never asked to create works for the Aldobrandinis? They pay extremely well. Why am I ignored? He seemed interested in my work when I met him at several of your dinners. I could paint an eight-pointed Aldobrandini star in a corner of one of my works as easily as the next artist.'

'We have quite enough Aldobrandini stars in Rome, thank you. In any case, am I not keeping you busy enough?' the Cardinal responds.

'Your Eminence, you have been kind and generous but work

from these others as well would help to cement my reputation. Why is it they never hire me?'

'I must be brutally honest, Michele. The Papal Nephew these days uses the talents of Annibale Carracci almost exclusively, and they say the cardinal is growing fond of landscapes, which you never paint. He said he found you arrogant, argumentative, intemperate. He labels you "artist as demiurge", a small-town upstart, a devil from the north. When he was interested in possibly offering you a commission, he had a trusted servant follow you for a day. The servant reported several ugly confrontations in Piazza Navona and a night of drinking and carousing in a tavern. You see, you have only yourself and your willful nature to blame. Lucky for you, I am willing to ignore all of that, to a certain point.'

'Yes, yes, but what did the Cardinal Nephew say of my painting?'

'He knows nothing of art. His only interest in painters is to glorify the reputation of the Aldobrandini family. Perhaps if your private life were not quite so boisterous, you would find more favour with him.'

———

As for his private life, Michele tries as best he can to keep this hidden from the cardinal and his servants, not wishing to be taken to task for his errant ways. But he senses that this freedom, this unalloyed licence, cannot last forever and will one day come to an end. He almost longs for that release and several days later, it is provided by the cardinal himself.

The cardinal has called Michele to his study. Michele wonders what this meeting could be about. The dark walls give the room a pleasant smell of old wood. Out the high windows, the cloud cover is breaking up to allow patches of azure to shine through.

As Michele enters, the cardinal looks up from his desk. 'A moment, please, I have some urgent papers to sign. As soon as I can give them to my servant, we can begin.'

Michele watches the cardinal scan the papers. The painter's mind drifts into a strange reverie. The painting of Saint Francis on the wall runs with glowing molten rivulets as on the slopes of a volcano. Out the window, the palaces and houses, monuments and churches glitter and shiver in the ever-changing light, the world inside and out is all surface, nothing but shimmering, multi-coloured surface.

The servant has come, taken the papers, and left. 'Excellent. Now, let us begin.' The cardinal stares at him, bringing Michele out of his reverie and back to the moment. 'For months now, Michele, I have not seen you in my chapel, not on Sunday or any other day. I trust you are fulfilling your weekly obligation at some other church in the city.' It could be taken as a statement but Michele understands it is clearly a question.

Michele remains silent, turns to stare out the window again. The silence stretches as the cardinal awaits an answer.

Finally, Del Monte says, 'My servants tell me that you are seldom here on a Saturday evening and you never return until the next afternoon. You have nothing to say in response?'

'Your Eminence, your spies have eyes to see but understand little. Do you wish to know where I spend my Saturday nights?'

'Yes, in fact, I do.'

'I am at the house of my courtesan. I must go to her place because, as you know, I cannot bring her here.'

'Ah, I see. Well, you are still young, I suppose it is to be expected. Her name?'

'Fillide Melandroni.'

'Ah, yes, I have heard of her. She is well-known about the city.'

'She is celebrated for good reason. I know you are a priest but I have no doubt you could appreciate skin like polished ivory, silken hair, a strong will, and a sense of humour. But above all, her voice intrigues me—even when I cannot see her, I can hear a smile in it. She adds a dramatic flair to my work.'

'To your work? What do you mean?'

'I have used her as a model in the past.'

'In which paintings?' the cardinal demands. 'In any of the works you have done for me?'

'She was my model for Saint Catherine of Alexandria.'

'Good Lord, Michele,' the cardinal exclaims in disbelief. 'You insist on treading dangerous ground.' He pauses and drums his fingers on the armrest of his chair, but then relents. 'But so it is.' He waves his hand at the air as if to dismiss the thought. 'I have come to realize it is your way, for whatever reason. And clearly a harlot can repent and attain sainthood. You have heard of Saint Theodota who did just that?'

'No. Theodota has escaped my notice, but if she was a harlot and later became a saint, perhaps I should do a painting of her using my Fillide as a model.'

'I suggest you refrain.'

'As you wish, Your Eminence. In any case, I truly appreciate your great understanding and sympathy.'

'Yes, I understand that, but I do not possess endless patience. I would prefer it not be known about the city and the Vatican that my artist places the image of a prostitute in my paintings.'

Michele is taken aback by the cardinal's reference to 'my paintings'. He refrains from saying that they remain 'his' paintings whoever commissions or owns them. Instead, he says, 'This question about my nights. You are jealous of my time, Your Eminence?'

'Not at all. But I am guarded with my reputation. A number of my cardinal colleagues have complained at the sensuousness in your works. I do tire of answering their charges and having to defend you.'

Michele nods. 'I see.' On the spot, he makes a decision. 'Perhaps it is time for me to move out.'

Cardinal Del Monte sighs. 'Perhaps you are right.'

Within a week, Michele and Mario have found living accommodations and a shared studio of reasonable size with Cardinal Mattei and his brother in their palazzo nearby, another patron eager to support the artist whose fame is spreading. Before leaving Palazzo Madama, Michele left Cardinal Del Monte a small painting of a lute player as a gift with a note: 'In appropriate recognition, I fervently hope, of the infinite favours and priceless confidence you have shown in me.'

For his part, the cardinal shows his considerable benevolence by continuing to try to arrange commissions for Michele with various churches throughout Rome, although Michele is gaining a reputation as an artist who refuses to follow the numerous details the church patrons set out for their paintings. Michele simply prefers to ignore the instructions about colours to use, and the figures and decorations to include. He might follow the dimensions required and the general subject matter but once he enters into a crucifixion or bloody martyrdom, brush and pigment take on a life of their own and he never knows beforehand what unusual direction the work will take. In fact, too many restrictions on any particular commission become a burden and he feels these strict instructions wrap him in chains. In most cases, he simply ignores them.

---

'I cannot go on with this, Mario. Look at it. I tire of painting figures as still lifes. I want to enter into the model's soul, tear out the model's heart, listen to it beating, feel it pulsing in my hand. There must be a better way.' Michele grabs a knife from the table next to his immense canvas with its life-sized images and is about to slash it when Mario hurries across the room from his own canvas, grips Michele's wrist and stops him.

'No!' he shouts, pulling Michele's hand down to his waist. 'You want too much. Let us go for a drink, get some air.'

'I do not want a drink. I want to paint.'

'A moment ago, you wanted to take a knife to it.'

'Look at them. These characters are stone, lifeless. I was in the Sistine yesterday, looking at the Adam there. Touched by the finger of God, he comes alive. Look at this Jesus before me. He is a hunk of marble dropped from the back of a cart.'

Michele leans down, elbows on knees, and stares at the floor. 'And something else is bothering me. That commission for a painting of the Holy Trinity for a church in Mexico has been given by the confraternity to Cavaliere d'Arpino. After they promised it to me. *Bastardi....*'

Mario sighs. 'I am sorry to hear that.' He contemplates the large painting on the easel. Michele has told him he is working on a depiction of the supper at Emmaus, when the resurrected Christ revealed Himself to two of his disciples and an innkeeper. And yet it remains a simple, everyday scene at a table. 'As for this work before us, may I make a suggestion?' Mario waits.

'Of course, Mario. You know I value your opinion.' He tosses the knife back onto the table and prepares to listen.

Mario pauses a moment. 'Go back in your thoughts to the scene in the Sistine Chapel you just mentioned. Picture the Adam there. Is God's finger actually touching his at the moment of Creation?'

'What do you mean?'

'Does the finger of God truly touch Adam's finger?'

Michele rubs his chin. 'No, it does not. You are correct. Michelangelo depicts the moment *before* they touch. The artist has left a slight space between their fingers.'

'Yes. That is where the life exists, the drama as you call it, that moment of intensity. The heart of the matter.' Mario turns again to Michele's painting. 'Look here, the man on the left sits like a lifeless lump of clay. Perhaps he should be about to rise from his chair. There should be more activity. Christ is resurrected, yes, but he is about to disappear from their lives forever. Expand the gestures. Open it up. The still life, that bowl of grapes, is gorgeous, glowing, a beautiful piece of work but is it enough? Let it add to the drama somehow. I am unsure how but I am certain you can think of something.'

Michele gazes at the bowl of grapes in the painting. 'You have given me an idea, Mario. I could place the bowl so it teeters at the edge of the table, overhanging it slightly, as if about to fall, as if everything in the lives of these people is about to change.'

———————

At a tavern near the Church of Santa Maria in Trastevere, Michele and Mario await their first plate. The artichokes that Michele ordered arrive and he discovers that half of them are cooked in butter instead of olive oil. Incensed, he hurls the plate of artichokes at the waiter, making a scene in the tavern and a mess across the floor and on the clothing of several other diners nearby. The waiter, a gangly fellow with long arms and the face of a dog, was not friendly to begin with and now he is seething, and reaching for his stiletto. Three other waiters in the establishment are hurrying over, scowls on their faces. Instead of staying to fight, as he normally would, Michele leaps for the door and flees into the night.

After running for several blocks, he realizes the waiters have given up their chase. Then a recent comment from Cardinal Mattei comes to him: *You will not stay here in my palazzo for long if you continue your scrapping ways on the streets of our city.*

Michele walks off his bad humour in a small grove of pine trees on the side of a hill a dozen streets away. A deep sigh lifts from his lungs and dissolves into the night air. He is sorry to have abandoned Mario to deal with the mess at the tavern, but he feels troubled, his heart uneasy. Michele steps out from the glade and tilts his head to the stars. Their sharp lights fill his eyes. He walks home.

On his arrival back at the palazzo, Mario is waiting. When Michele enters, Mario confronts him, 'Why are you angry all the time? Your art is well received, your income has increased considerably, Fillide is happy to spend time with you, and you have the best of friends in me.' Mario smiles, trying to lighten the mood.

'Why am I always angry? Where shall I begin? Everything disappoints. Fillide spends too much time with other men. Because they have family names long recognized in Rome, everyone in this district bows down to them and treats them like royalty. I should split their skulls open, one by one. As well, I begin to suspect I will never master my art, never fully become the artist I desire to be.'

'That is surely not true,' Mario insists, shaking his head. 'I have seen you at work on a painting. Nothing else exists at that moment. You seem to enter into another world, the world of the painting. You live inside the work until it is done. Do you realize you cannot talk of anything else but the painting you are working on, whichever it is, even when we go out to eat and drink? Meanwhile, you are considered a master by numerous artists in Rome and by patrons of art in the city. Look at me. I have sold one painting in the past year and yet I persist. I wonder at the source of your unhappiness. Not just unhappiness, but bitterness. If a young scoundrel on the piazza mocks your work, you seize your rapier and are ready to open his gut. And you sulk for a week and want to cut up whatever canvas you are working on at the moment. Who cares what the fools say?'

―――――――

Several days later, Cardinal Mattei calls Michele to his room. His Eminence is a pious man. Piety seems to ooze from his pores, and he can barely look Michele in the eye. With a small gesture, he bids Michele take a seat. The cardinal holds a sheet of paper in his shaking hand. 'A contact of mine at court his given me some testimony that was taken yesterday from one Antonio de Madii of Piacenza, employed as a copyist.'

'I don't know him.'

'Of course not. Allow me to read it to you. The signor from

Piacenza stated, "I was having dinner at the Tavern of the Blackmoor. On the other side of the room was Michelangelo Merisi, the painter. I heard him ask the waiter whether the artichokes were done in oil or butter, they being all in one plate. The waiter said, 'I don't know,' and picked one up and put it to his nose. The painter took it amiss, sprang to his feet in rage, and shouted, 'You damned cuckold, you think you are serving some bum!' He then seized the plate with the artichokes and threw it in the waiter's face. I did not see Merisi grasp his sword to threaten the waiter."' The cardinal pauses and raises his tired, basilisk eyes from the page to look at Michele sitting before him. 'What do you have to say about this?'

'Your Eminence, as it says, I did not draw my sword. No charges have been laid.'

'A miracle,' Cardinal Mattei mutters with mild sarcasm. 'No charges, this time. But I fear one day you will lose your temper entirely and go too far. Beware that day, Michele. It will be your end.'

# ⊰ THE ASSASSIN ⊱

---

I toss and turn on my mat, sweating through the bedclothes after an evening of drink. My head heavy, my guts churn with raw wine. A dream comes to me. I stand on the Ponte Sant'Angelo, staring down at the river whose flow is sluggish and whose colour resembles a rat's slick coat.

'Luca, Luca,' I hear a half-strangled voice calling me. Turning around, I confront the severed head of Enzo Rondini atop a post slick with gore. I do not question how it is that Rondini can speak with his throat cut through.

'What do you want with me, Rondini?'

'This could be you up here.'

'I am aware of that. But, thank you for not giving me away under torture for the several murders we committed together.'

'You believe I am a man of honour? Do not be a fool. I am no Saint Paul whose decapitated head bounced three times to reveal three springs. No gush of cleansing water here, only blood. In any case, there was a long line of others I much preferred to name before you. My executioners never gave me the chance to get around to you, Luca.'

I wonder if he will mention the fact that I cheated him of his share of coin for the murder of Peretti.

I have my answer immediately. 'I know you kept more than half of the gold coins from our last crime together.'

'No, no, not gold; merely silver.'

'How would I know if it was silver or gold, having not seen my share? I should have given you up.'

'But you refrained. Clearly, you are no Judas.'

'And you are no Jesus, nor any kind of saint. No, I will never understand why I refused to betray you.'

Suddenly, in the dream I stand at the end of the bridge looking back at the row of mounted heads. Rondini's is twice the size of the others and is mouthing something to me. I draw closer and stand in front of him again. 'What is it?'

'This could be you up here.'

'I know that. Stop repeating the same thing.' I clutch my ears with my hands.

'This could be you. Up here. Your neck running with blood, eyes bulging, your tongue hanging down. Listen, Luca, pluck out one of my eyes and keep it in your pocket. I will watch out for your enemies and protect you.'

I begin to reach for my dagger but stop on hearing a cackling laugh coming from Rondini. He is mocking me.

'Luca, I am saving you a place in Hell.'

———————

That afternoon, the sound of a crow cawing from a nearby roof passes through my head like black lightning and I awake. I feel as if waves have been pounding my body against rock all night, I am abandoned on a beach of stones, crabs scratching through the gravel of my brain, a ball of eels squirming in my guts.

I drag myself out of sleep and try to walk it off. Outside, the heat is intense. Everywhere, the annoying sound of cicadas scratches and rasps on the air. I tread along the Tiber, glorying in the rough texture of my hangover. My head pounds and I've retched by the side of the river three times. I can't eat and I'm a bit dizzy, but I love this feeling of baseness, of dragging myself through the muck. The swamp of my past has disappeared; the dark, stinking sewer that is my future is invisible. I can think of nothing right now but my ruined, tortured body and I can say it is a strange kind of relief to have my thoughts so focused and limited.

But eventually, as I shamble along, I start feeling a little improvement. I am walking to nowhere because the painter doesn't want me to model today, hasn't needed me for a week. I tire of him, and I can tell he grows tired of me. It can be heard in the way he talks to me of late. Another short spell of friendliness is over. He said maybe next week he would need me for a day only. I am badly in need of money.

As I shuffle along on this hot day, I notice there are no boys swimming. The sodomite-burning Pope has banned nude swimming in the river. No more lithe youngsters slipping in and out of the stream like water rats.

I pass under a bridge, and who should be sitting there in the shade but Carlo the Ear, from the tavern.

'Friend,' I greet him.

He is half-drunk, sweating, hands me a bottle of wine, the dregs of which taste like piss. 'Friend? Only your friend when you need something from me, and you're *my* friend only when you are paying me good coin for the information I give you. So, what do you need today, Luca?'

Not far off, two old men stand with their fishing lines in the water, one dead fish at their feet. More bone than flesh. The fish, that is. But as I gaze at them, I see they too are skin and bone under their thin, washed-out shirts. More to the point, they are far enough off not to be able to hear us.

'Work,' I say, 'Work, Carlo. Real work that pays good coin. I need to know who in the city is seeking revenge and is willing to pay well for it. Who has had his honour insulted?'

'Ah, that kind of work.'

I sit down next to him on the stones. My head pounds. I notice he stinks, worse than me.

'That kind of work does not come along every day. I know of nothing now but, count on it, there will be something soon.

There always is. Of course, information of that sort is worth more than a few scudi. It comes at a cost.'

'What kind of cost?'

'One half of what you are paid for the job, when it comes.'

'One half? Outrageous.'

'It's your choice, Luca. You can keep one-half of something or enjoy the whole of nothing. It is up to you. Come see me next week at my tavern.'

## ⊰ THE ARTIST ⊱

Each time Michele goes out into the street, to the tennis courts, or to Piazza Navona or one of the other piazzas he frequents, he is promptly recognized as 'the famous painter from Lombardy'. He takes pride in this recognition but it brings problems as well. His enemies, mostly certain other artists, too, recognize him and taunt him without mercy.

One evening, as he and Mario cross Piazza Navona, the air high above crisscrossed by hundreds of swallows, Livio and several of his friends see them. The insults start immediately. 'Ah, if it isn't Michele the sodomite!' Livio shouts at him. 'With his bumboy in tow.' Livio glances around at his friends. 'Fraud. Impostor,' one of them barks, 'a painter of no talent. Look at him strutting about like a rooster, believing he's the Emperor of Rome when he is simply the lackey of cardinals, a servant boy, his arse in the air. The *great* painter—not even a true Roman.'

Another in the crowd taunts Michele directly: 'You paint with two left hands.'

A third proclaims, 'No, no. Look at the paintings. He uses his cock as his brush!' Everyone laughs. Encouraged, he goes on: 'And Fillide the whore is the pot into which he dips it!'

At first Michele and Mario ignore them, but that last comment about Fillide stings. When Livio and three of his friends block Michele and Mario's passage as they try to enter a tavern, Michele draws his rapier. He does it with an unhurried deliberation that he hopes will show he is only warning them. He fears his new patron would not be pleased to hear that his painter has been involved in yet another brawl.

One of Livio's gang steps in front and also pulls his rapier. 'If you want to fight, scum, you will have to fight me, and you will *not* be walking away as a whole man. Your whore will have a hard time finding what she's looking for.'

'Who the hell are you?' Michele scowls. The man staring at Michele has the dead eyes of a dog on the hunt and nostrils that flare. He grips his rapier so tightly his knuckles turn white.

'My name is Ranuccio Tomassoni, a name you are not soon to forget.' Michele recognizes the family name but not the familiar. He recalls that the Tomassoni men are soldiers, recently returned to Rome to cause endless trouble. *This must be the youngest of the brood.*

'Wait.' Another member of Livio's crowd slinks forward and eases down Tomassoni's rapier. He is a short, wide-shouldered young painter from Florence named Giorgio. Michele knows him slightly. Another hot-head but one whose painting Michele rather admires. 'You know what the problem is with this Michele?' he asks the surrounding crowd that has gathered to watch. 'He lacks the skill for painting ears on his figures. All the ears he paints end up looking exactly alike.'

The crowd laughs. Mario comes to Michele's defence: 'You lie through your throat! Of course he can paint ears. He does a fine job with them.'

'Oh, he can paint ears all right, it is just that they all look the same.'

Michele shakes his head in exasperation, and at that moment, a phalanx of police arrives to break up the crowd and put an end to the impending fight.

As Michele and Mario make their way into the tavern, Michele appears thoughtful, brooding, staring at the ground.

'What is it?' Mario asks. 'What has gotten to you?'

Michele glances at his friend. 'He had it right, you know, that painter. I have seen and admired his work. He has a fine eye. All the ears I paint do look similar. I pay little attention to them. I did not believe they were important. I never thought anyone would notice.'

---

Morning light spills into the room. The heavy, meaty, animal smell of sex fills the air. The remains of their meal from the night before that Michele picked up from a taverna litters a table: crusts of bread, two cups with dregs of wine, some bones from stewed meat on a plate.

The objects on another small dressing table reveal Fillide's success as a well-paid courtesan: a small oval mirror with several jars of scented oils and creams before it, a fan, a box of inlaid tortoiseshell for jewellery, two ivory combs, a terracotta doll from the city of Lucca and a rosary of amber.

Fillide rolls on her side and throws her arm across Michele's chest, gazing up at him. 'Tell me, what are you thinking?'

'Since you ask, I will tell you—I had a conversation several nights past with Cardinal Del Monte's brother. He has written a book on perspective. We talked a long while about anamorphosis.'

'What is that?' She strokes his chest, running her fingers through the hairs.

'A special way of drawing a figure with distortion so that it appears normal when viewed from a certain angle. I am considering using it in one of my church commissions where the viewer is forced to observe the painting from a difficult perspective because the painting will be installed in a narrow side-chapel. In any case, he raised questions for me, not only about perspective but about perception itself.'

'What do you mean?'

'Do you really enjoy discussing such philosophical subjects or are you trying to humour me?'

'You consider me stupid because I am a woman and a courtesan.'

'No, not at all, Fillide. You have it wrong. You are the most sharp-witted woman I have ever known. It is one of the things I love about you. And, let me add, there are other things I love about you as well.'

'Do not talk to me of love. I cannot afford love. If I was meant to have love, my father would not have died when I was young and left me with no dowry. But do tell me about the questions that disturb your mind.'

'Yes, about perception. If we cannot trust our eyes to reveal the world as it is, then what is real? If our gaze can be manipulated and controlled, is what we see what is actually there, or are we simply seeing those things we already know, and have seen before, and are we missing everything else?'

'You are right, let us not talk philosophy.' She rolls away from him. After a short silence, she says, 'The day of your birth is September 29, is it not?'

'Yes, that is true.'

'Who is your patron saint?'

'Michael the Archangel.'

'O, such an exalted patron. An archangel, no less.'

'Not so. I was intrigued to learn he is the patron saint of death. And I feel more fallen angel than archangel, blown in every direction by the wind.'

'If last night's performance in this bed, added to this morning's, are any indication, you are no angel.' She laughs lightheartedly and lifts the covers. 'Ah, I see why you like to talk philosophy. If we go again, I will have to charge you double.'

'Slut. You have discovered my great weakness. But I love you anyway.'

She fingers the silver amulet on a chain around her neck.

He half rolls over toward her, moves her long dark hair out of the way and takes the twisted, horn-shaped amulet in his fingers. 'Beautiful. Expensive no doubt. I have never seen you wear it before. You did not remove it all night. Where did you get it?'

'It is for warding off the evil eye. A gift from an admirer.'

'It must be someone you feel strong affection for if you keep it on at all times.'

She remains silent and Michele takes this to mean he is correct. 'Who is it?'

'Are you jealous? You know I have customers other than you.'

'Am I just another customer, then? I was hoping not . . .'

'No. I must admit that you are my light and my joy. If I were ever to stop this work, if I could afford to do so, I would surely spend the rest of my life with you. Would you like that?'

'Would I like that? I would love it, and I truly hope the future holds such a fate for us.' He pauses. 'Now, who gave you such an expensive gift. Who?'

'I fear to say. Not because I love him but because I know you have a temper and will cause pain and trouble for yourself if you know his name. And, because I truly do love you, I do not want you to cause such pain for yourself.'

'I see you have made up your mind.' Michele leaps out of bed and starts getting dressed. 'I must go.'

She says nothing but sits watching him. He too remains silent.

As he is pulling on his shoes and preparing to leave, she says, 'I will tell you because I do trust you. Promise me you will not act against him.' She pauses, then whispers, 'His name is Ranuccio.'

He doesn't look at her but mumbles as he leaves, 'I'll tear his life out of his throat.'

She throws her head back on the bed, realizing her terrible mistake.

———————

Several highly-ranked clerics, as well as a few artists, art collectors and intellectuals, have been invited by Cardinal Del Monte to view a new ornate mechanism the cardinal has received, a clock from France. The group, including the cardinal's brother, Guidubaldo, crowd about the new object.

About the size of a man's torso, the clock rests on a round table in the middle of the drawing room so that the guests can observe the marvel from all angles. The complexity of its inner workings can be viewed through glass panels on three sides while the elegant clock is open and accessible from the back.

'It is made by a jeweler in Paris,' the cardinal explains. 'His name is Jules Belmonde.'

The guests saunter around the table, some coming close to observe the works inside, others standing back simply to enjoy the clock as an object of art. Without a doubt, it is a thing of beauty, with a pair of gold-leafed Doric columns beside the round face, and a bell in the shape of Saint Peter's dome on top.

'It is exquisite, yes, but what is unusual about it?' Michele asks.

The cardinal replies. 'Look at the hands. Most unusually, there are two. It has what Belmonde calls a "minute" hand, allowing the clock to reveal the segments of an hour as it passes.'

The guests nod their heads, impressed. They have never before seen a clock that keeps such precise time.

Michele strides to the back of the clock and leans forward, his right hand resting on the wooden table. As he studies the works of the clock, the major-domo, Lorenzo, standing behind him, drolly remarks, 'I suspect the French have a larger version by which they punish criminals, casting them in to be chewed up by the gears.'

The cardinal scowls at his steward and Lorenzo takes a step back. Meanwhile, Michele fixes his gaze on the heart of the apparatus, open to view at the back of the clock, and sees the gears turn as the passing of the minute is executed. Sticking the index finger of his left hand into the clock, he believes he can feel the pulse of time passing. With his finger he explores the inner workings of the clock. Just then, the gears that control the hour hand click, ratchet down, and catch Michele's finger in the works. It takes him until the bell has finished ringing three times to mark the hour before he can remove the injured finger. Drops of blood from its tip drip to the floor.

Lorenzo steps forward with a clean handkerchief he has pulled from his pocket, saying, 'As if a lizard hides within, yes?' He hands the cloth to the artist, who takes it and wraps his finger, squeezing it tight.

---

On Wednesday of Easter Week, a pleasant spring sun brightens the sky after several days of cleansing rain. Michele has been working hard for several weeks and, as usual at this point, he is about to explode and is spoiling for a fight to break the intensity. He decides to go out and walk with Mario to the piazza fronting the Basilica Santa Maria Maggiore. They know the Pope will be stopping there as it is one of the seven pilgrim churches of Rome he will visit on this day during Holy Week. They figure it will be a lively scene with the colourful pageantry of the Pope's procession. Michele is hoping to find and confront one of his many enemies, particularly Ranuccio Tomassoni, among the expected crowds. Every sinew and muscle in his body is longing to burst forth and relieve itself in struggle.

They stand in the middle of the piazza and wait. In front of the church, a doomsayer, head tilted back as he gazes into heaven with blank eyes, harangues a small crowd: 'Romans, listen to me! There will be suffering and weeping and tribulation among you. The day is upon us. Yesterday a two-headed calf was born in a farm village to the south. A swarm of silver butterflies, thick enough to blot out the sun, appeared above a church in a town to the north. These are signs, Romans. Pay heed!'

The attention of the two friends is drawn away from the man as they hear chanting and notice a crowd of clergy, soldiers and cardinals in scarlet robes as the papal procession approaches from a nearby street. The pilgrimage is led by a flag-bearer holding high the banner displaying the coat of arms of the Albobrandinis, the Pope's family, with its six, eight-pointed stars. The Aldobrandinis are the family that Michele longs to connect with, to start gaining their interest and receiving their substantial commissions. As the procession floods into the piazza and the Pope's carriage appears, another procession, a funeral cortege, enters from a second nearby street.

Michele quickly scans the crowds and sees none of his enemies present. No fighting today but perhaps he can fill his eyes with colour and escape for a while the present work weighing on him back in his studio.

'Look.' He points. 'The eagle over a dragon, the arms of the Borghese. These two families are long-time foes. They despise each other.' He smiles at the possible confrontation.

The Borghese cortege, also led by a phalanx of clerics, includes an open bier pulled by two majestic, caparisoned horses. On top of the bier rests a Borghese notable, his corpse wrapped in purple cloth.

As the two processions meet in the piazza, members from each group warn the others to move and make way. 'The Holy Father must pass' and 'We have a funeral to attend' and 'Move along now' and 'The Borghese chapel is in the basilica, let us pass,' are phrases tossed back and forth. Then several marchers begin to shout.

'Ah, perhaps there will be a fight after all,' Michele says to Mario as he steps forward. But no fight ensues. Both groups back off and make their way around each other.

The two friends have been watching the crowd before them. Finally, Michele says, 'I don't see the *cazzo* I was looking for. Let's go.'

As the two friends head down an alley, they notice that the doomsayer they had seen on the church steps earlier is trudging along ahead of them.

Michele turns to Mario. 'Let us stop him and see if he will tell our fortune.'

Mario shakes his head and waves his hands. 'No, no. I don't want to know my future.'

Ignoring his friend, Michele increases his pace and catches up to the prophet. 'Doomsayer,' he calls. 'Stop a moment and tell my future, will you? I've got a solid scudo for you if you agree. You will be able to afford meat and wine tonight.'

The man stops and turns. The grey rags and hood he wears could have been found on a rubbish heap. In the nest of their darkness his eyes burn bright. He appears to stare past them into some unfathomable distance. 'Meat? Who said meat?'

Michele approaches. 'Will you tell my fortune for a coin?'

The doomsayer seems to see him for the first time, lowers his gaze, and focuses. 'Yes, I can do that. These eyes see all, clearly and without blemish. The coin.' He sticks out his palm.

Michele digs into his small purse and pulls out a scudo, hands it to the man who takes it, stares at it a moment and shoves it deep in his pocket. The man then turns his head far to the right, as if he sees something there. He pauses, thinking, then speaks. 'You … are a man of pain. You have seen how, during Carnival, Jews are forced to run naked down the Via del Corso, in cold or rain, all the while the Romans pelting them with stones and garbage. And last month, you remember when the rains never ceased and the clerics blamed the bad weather on the burial of a Jew in consecrated ground and how dozens of young scoundrels ran to the graveyard and dug him up and scattered his bones about the streets? You recall that? You will be one of those miserable Jews. The Pope won't even allow you to read your Torah.'

'But I am no Jew,' Michele replies, confused.

'Nevertheless, like any Jew, you will be anathema. God's grace will abandon you. I repeat, you are a man of pain, a wanderer.'

Michele shakes his head and waves the doomsayer away.

'Do not listen to him,' Mario warns as they wander off. 'He simply wanted his coin. He is mad.'

But Michele walks in silence for a long while. Even when Mario tries to cheer him by saying, 'Today is a holy day. Perhaps the cardinal's kitchen will serve us veal for dinner,' it has no effect on his mood.

## ⊲{ THE ASSASSIN }⊳

The next week, as arranged, I hurry to the tavern where Carlo the Ear spends his time. He waits for customers in his usual seat, far across the noisy room, his back against the wall. I make my way there, nodding to a few familiar faces on my way as I avoid a drunk passed out on the floor.

'Greetings,' Carlo says. He sits tall and straight before a jug of wine so I know he is drunk.

I pull up a chair. 'What have you found for me?'

He takes a long draught from his cup, wipes his mouth with the back of his hand and glances across the room. 'Nothing of the sort of work you seek. But I will keep listening.' He pauses. 'Something else ...'

'What? What is it?'

He waits a moment, in silence, then explains.

'A few days ago, there was a man here, not one of "us". He was dressed like one of us, and tried to act like one of us, but he was clearly not one of us. He was asking too many questions.'

'What sort of questions?'

'Questions about Signore Claudio Peretti, the wealthy patron who got himself murdered.'

Luca pauses, wishing that he could leave. 'Why should that concern me?'

'O, it should concern you, if you value your neck.'

'That has nothing to do with me. Not one of my jobs.' I know that Carlo recognizes a lie when he hears one.

'As you wish.' Carlo tilts his head back and polishes off his cup, pours himself more from the jug. 'In any case, let me put it this way, Luca. I said nothing to this man about you. I cannot say for sure if your hands are covered with Peretti's blood or not, but I have my suspicions. I suspect that when you were here asking about Rondini after his arrest, that is what you were getting at.' Carlo is sober now, eyeing me with a hard look. 'A single word to this fellow could send him prying about in your direction. Do you wish that?' He taps the wooden table hard with his knobby index finger and raises his bushy eyebrows. 'In the past you have paid for my information. Now you will pay for my silence.'

———————

The next day, I happen to be passing the French Church of San Luigi. Merisi told me this is the church where the painting in which he used me as a model has been hung. In the Contarelli Chapel, he said. I decide to enter, curious to see myself on the walls of a church.

I have been reluctant to enter churches since I realized I was a man destined for Hell. This one intimidates me. It looks rich, with colourful paintings all over the walls and ceiling and its huge columns. It shines with gold, this church. Why should the priests have so much wealth, the fattened clergy living in splendour when people like me are starving?

I have no trouble finding the chapel in question. It is a small side chapel with a ceiling that looks like the inside of a barrel.

Three paintings are there. The smallest one, *Matthew and the Angel*, is in the middle above a narrow altar, with two black marble columns framing it. *The Calling of Saint Matthew* on the left dwarfs it, as does the *Martyrdom of Matthew* on the right. The window above the altar lets in light at an angle that echoes the light in the artist's painting of *The Calling*.

How strange to see myself here in this painting, a murderer soaked in blood in a church of God. The Pope and his cardinals would be livid if they knew who Merisi had used as his Matthew. They would no doubt have the work removed and burned, and the artist thrown in prison for heresy or sacrilege. Perhaps I can threaten the artist that I will mention to Del Monte or Cardinal Mattei that he has used a criminal as a model for this painting. Perhaps Merisi will pay for my silence, as I have been forced to pay Carlo. Of course, why would I mention my own crimes to a prelate who might pass the knowledge on to the authorities? Not such a good plan after all. Besides, Del Monte is intent on doing everything he can to protect the artist. But at some point, there must be a way to shake a few coins out of this outrage— me, a great sinner, one damned as surely as Judas himself, playing an apostle of Jesus, installed permanently in a church of God. What a desecration, what sacrilege!

But it feels good to see my face up there on the wall. I turn and look about. The church is empty, not even an old hag deep in her paternosters or a bent servant sweeping the floors. Perhaps I can grab something while I'm here. A chalice of gold? Something with jewels that I can tear off? I check around the side chapel. Nothing on this little altar. As I step out into the nave to sidle up to the main altar in search of portable treasure, a priest comes sweeping out from a side door and hurries down the two steps leading to the altar area.

'Can I be of assistance? Have you come for confession?'

I turn and run.

# ⚜ THE ARTIST ⚜

---

Rome is sweltering. Long days of heat in early July have wrapped the city in a fog of sweat. The streets are empty at midday, and crowded at night when no one can sleep. Fights break out for no reason, random sparks from a chisel hacking marble.

Michele slouches in his chair across the studio from Mario, who is painting.

He and Mario did not last long at the palazzo of Cardinal Mattei, but Michele now has enough money to rent his own lodgings. He stares at his friend. *How can he paint? How can he even move? It is so damnably hot I cannot stand. The air has a weight that is impossible to lift. My body is a wet bag.* His head sags between his knees and then he hauls it up again. *He paints like a mason laying bricks.* He struggles to his feet and labours over to Mario.

'Look, here,' he says, pointing to the Madonna that Mario is painting. 'Put in more azurite along here, and there, and here. Lighten it here, darken it there. You need more contrast.'

Mario pauses and listens as Michele goes on. 'The angel there, very pretty, winsome. But the age of angels and heavenly saints is over. Angels only exist in Bible stories and dreams. And every saint was once a man or woman who had great temptations to overcome. That's where the drama exists, that's where the true art lies—in that struggle between light and dark, never knowing which will win out. Believe me, Mario, I learned long ago in my youth that to live a life of brilliance, one must first descend into the depths of darkness.'

Mario frowns at Michele who now feels badly. He knows his comments will remind Mario who is the more successful painter. Although he has completed his apprenticeship, Mario has gained no commissions since arriving in Rome, and his work is ignored by patrons and the public alike. The single painting Mario sold in the past year brought in little money, and he has no other source of income. Michele does not mind supporting him, though he knows it must wear on the younger man's self-respect and confidence.

'My apologies, Mario. It's this damnable heat. I can't stand it. We never had heat like this back home, up north. How can you paint in the middle of the day?'

'I am from Sicily. This is nothing. I remember afternoons at home so hot that the weeds in the fields would burst into flame when a faint, dry breeze rubbed them together.'

Michele motions languidly toward a side table cluttered with paints and brushes. 'A letter came for you.'

Mario hurries to the table, snatches up the letter, and reads it. At first his face is blank as he wipes sweat from his brow, then he leans forward and looks more intent. Suddenly his eyes brighten and he smiles.

Michele hovers nearby, contemplating Mario's canvas. Finally, Mario looks up, waving the letter. 'It is from Sicily. My uncle.'

'Yes?' Michele can tell he has important news to disclose.

'Can you believe it? By the grace of God, he has found me a commission, a large one, in his local church near Palermo.'

'Will you go?'

Mario pauses, lowers the letter to his thigh. 'This is exactly what I have been waiting for. Yes, I believe I will. I'll leave in several weeks. Rome has not brought me the success I expected. Despite all my efforts, I am failing here.'

He carefully refolds the letter and returns it to its envelope, which he places in the pocket of his painter's smock, patting it tenderly once it's safe.

————————

'Mario, give me a hand with this ladder.' Michele stands at the door to their studio, holding a long ladder.

'Of course, of course. Where did you find it and what is it for?'

'I noticed it in the alley behind and snatched it while the landlady is out. I'm sure she will wonder why I need a ladder and I don't want to tell her. Let us hurry before she returns.'

Mario grabs one end of the ladder and they move it into the studio and set it up. 'Once again, what are you doing?'

Michele points at the painting he's working on. 'I need a more direct beam of light. I'm going to cover the windows and make a hole in the roof so I can bring sunlight right down onto the canvas.'

Michele snatches a hammer from his worktable and scurries up the ladder. He starts pounding at the roof and soon has a ragged hole cut open. He stops and looks at it. 'Perfect,' he says.

He climbs down. 'Now help me get this ladder back to its place before she returns.'

———————

After several thunderstorms with heavy rain, the landlady notices the water dripping from his rooms down to the first floor and investigates while Michele is out. She then complains to Michele about the hole. 'Why? Why make a hole in the roof of my house?!'

'I need to let the light in for my painting,' he says, an explanation which not only displeases her but confuses her as well.

The landlady, middle-aged and sturdy, keeps wiping her hands on her apron, though there is no flour or oil on them. 'The room has windows for light! I am forced to bear a complaint against you and take you to court. The entire neighbourhood knows of your bad reputation. Three weeks ago, you move into my house and I provide you a large room on the upper floor as a painter's studio. Like a crazy man, you pound a hole in the ceiling of the room. In a perfectly good roof.'

Michele does not show the least shred of embarrassment.

She continues. 'You must offer to fix my roof or pay to have it fixed.'

'Let me explain. I need a dark room for my painting, with a strong streak of light angling in from above. This is the only way I can obtain the particular effect I require. I am working on an important painting for Cardinal Del Monte. I used to be a member of his household,' he adds, thinking that, once again, it might help his case to mention his past relationship with the well-known cardinal.

'But clearly you are no longer a member of his household as you now have your own lodgings.'

'It is true.'

The landlady thinks a moment. 'If you take it upon yourself to fix the roof, I will not take you to court. Do you understand?'

'Yes.'

Later that day, Michele hammers together a wooden cover, mounts the ladder and passes it through the oval-shaped hole. It is a removable cap, so whenever he wants to paint, he can climb the ladder, lift the wooden cover up onto the roof, and capture his precious beam of light. Later, when he has finished for the day, he can ascend the ladder again, replace the cover and keep out all but the worst weather. The landlady remains displeased with the situation, a frown darkening her face every time she sees him, but she makes no further fuss about it.

---

Michele drags his worktable into the brightness and moves his paints, pots of linseed oil, and his brushes off to one side. As he pulls his rapier from its scabbard, he enjoys the slight metallic swish that the sword makes on being drawn, the steel whisper that signals imminent action, an impending brawl.

He places the rapier on the worktable, where the light hits it. He runs his hand along the blade. The hilt swirls in a complex of metal tracery. The light slides along the rapier's length. It seems alive. He has felt it jump in his hand, leap and thrust on its own. He barely needs to consider how to move or manoeuvre when he holds it in a street fight.

He suspects he might need his rapier tonight, for his friend, Onorio Longhi, has returned to Rome from the wars up north. They are to meet later at the tennis courts. Onorio loves a good fight and will certainly be spoiling for action this evening. When he and Michele are together, it seems as if two gusts of wind join forces and begin to feed each other. Michele admits to himself that he would be thrilled to engage in brawling tonight if he sees any of his rivals on the street, especially Ranuccio Tomassoni.

As he stares at the sword, he notices a faint blush of rust on the forte, up near the hilt. Taking a rag dipped in linseed oil, he wipes at the corrosion. He is able to remove most of it, but he has to apply more pressure and use the hard-stitched edge of the rag to remove it entirely. Having done that, he dips more oil and strokes a thin layer along the rapier's length. Taking a dry rag in hand, he wipes off any extra oil, polishing as he goes.

A close inspection along the two blade edges reveals no nicks, so he decides to sharpen the rapier. Placing a rectangular sharpening stone on the table, he drips oil on its surface and spreads it out with the side of his thumb. Then he strokes the edge of the blade over it at about a thirty-degree angle. First one side of the rapier, then the other. He does this over and over until he is satisfied with the way it looks and the smooth, sandy hiss it makes as it passes over the stone. He takes another rag, dips it in water, and runs it carefully along each edge of the blade, and then dries it thoroughly.

Lifting the rapier, he looks along its length. He slides his thumb lightly along the blade to test for sharpness, a procedure he has performed a thousand times before. This time, without his even feeling the blade slicing into his thumb, he sees the instant welling of blood from the slit. *Just like the clock*, he thinks. *Why is my world constantly attacking me?*

---

'Cecco? He is my new apprentice. That is all.'

'And, this young boy, he lives with you?' Fillide shakes her head, trying to understand.

'Yes, of course, it's a common thing. An apprentice often lives with the artist who is training him. Just as Mario did. But Mario has returned to Sicily. Cecco comes from Lombardy. Our families know each other, and his father asked that I take him on and teach him the painter's trade. This spring I see several commissions coming my way. I need an assistant to grind pigments, ready canvas and do various tasks.'

'I'm not sure I believe you.' Fillide pokes Michele in his bare chest. Michele notes that her hands, in particular, seem much older than the rest of her, long-fingered and wrinkled, like the hands of an ancient washerwoman.

'It's the truth. He's a quick learner. More attentive than I was at his age.'

'Does he share your bed?' She lowers her eyes, light falling on her bare shoulder, skin glowing.

'Of course not. I only share my bed with you. Why do you want to know? Are you jealous?'

'Hah, you don't want to tell me because you love him.'

Michele gazes at the back of his hand. 'I suppose I do love him, in a way. Like a father loves his son.'

'You expect me to believe that?'

'You will believe what you want to believe, in any case.'

'Be careful, my love. I was out walking with Ranuccio the other night...'

'I don't want to hear about it.'

'O, but I think you do. We were joined by a servant he knows named Lorenzo, from Cardinal Del Monte's retinue. His head servant, I believe. You know him?'

'Unfortunately, yes.'

'I didn't like him at all. They began discussing a painting you did in which Cecco was the model for Cupid. This Lorenzo mentioned that Cecco is a well-known plaything for sodomites in the quarter.'

'Does that bother you?'

'Not at all. But I heard them conspiring to report you to the authorities, to claim you are a sodomite. They clearly hate you. Lorenzo is leaving the cardinal's service and wants to give you this parting gift. I don't think they've reported you yet. But don't blame Ranuccio. It is all the fault of that Lorenzo. He plans to leave service next month. What will you do?'

'I don't know. Why should I not blame Ranuccio? He clearly despises me.' Michele bites his lip and stares at the floor. 'Now it is my turn to ask you—do you love him?'

'No. Absolutely not. I love only you, my darling, only you. I am considering stopping servicing other men because I love you. But I need the money. If I stop, I will soon starve.'

Michele looks up, smiling. 'I know what I'll do. I'll move in with you and we will live as man and wife. Perhaps I can find a priest willing to marry us for a scudo or two.'

'Hah,' she scoffs. 'My sweet pet, I have no dowry to bring to the marriage, as you know, and I have no doubt you would run off at the first sign of a dropped handkerchief from some pretty young maiden.'

'Never.' He grins. 'I love you, Fillide. Someday soon, I believe we will be together for good. And I believe that you believe that too.'

'I do. I do believe that. Not right now, but soon. You are a wonderful sinner, a good man and a marvellous artist. Come here.' She puts her hand behind his head and pulls his face down to her breasts.

———————

Michele trudges back to his rooms after spending the evening getting drunk with friends at a tavern. He hopes to find Cecco at home. The hour is late and the streets in his area are empty and unlit. He turns a corner and there in the middle of the street stands a mongrel staring at him. Michele hesitates, not knowing if the dog is about to attack. But the dog doesn't move. It stares at him with a look of profound sadness, then slinks down an alley and disappears.

As Michele continues on his way, he reflects on what his life has come to in the last several years since leaving Cardinal Del Monte's palazzo. Mario has gone home to Sicily—Michele has received several letters from his friend who is working hard on his painting, with some success. Del Monte, continuing his loyalty to Michele, has helped him secure another church commission. Meanwhile, several private collectors are avid to purchase his paintings as fast as he can produce them.

They pay well, these patricians with a taste for art. The banker Vincenzo Guistiniani, and others, such as the Contarelli family. Michele is pleased that he can paint whatever he wants for the private collectors. He even painted a highly erotic frontal nude of Cecco that, at the time, he feared might bring him trouble. And perhaps it has, now that Fillide has told him of the threat from Lorenzo. But they loved it, Guistiniani and all his rich, tasteful friends. He cannot be so daring with the church commissions, of course. The clerics want biblical scenes for their churches—saints, martyrs, the holy family, and on and on. Michele doesn't mind these—they make him consider how to present a complex scene, and sometimes these paintings of saints and church history turn out to be daringly secular as they flow from Michele's brush. He skirts a dangerous edge. His whole life has been about edging along a precipice, the abyss always one step away. He knows he is creating art unlike anything being done in Rome or elsewhere. He paints *what* he wants to paint and *how* he wants to paint. The rules do not apply to him, not in art, not in life. This view gets him into endless trouble, of course, but he has no choice. To compromise his art, to betray his talents, would cause him to wither and die.

The street funnels into a dimmer alley. He notices someone in the distance ahead, leaning against a wall. As he draws near, a man steps out into the middle of the alley and speaks, hand resting on the hilt of his sword.

'Michelangelo Merisi, is it?'

Michele recognizes the voice, and then the face, of Ranuccio Tomassoni. A hot coal flares inside his head.

'Tomassoni. What do you want? Waiting to ambush me in the street?'

'No ambush. I am here to warn you, so you can savour how I am about to bring you down.'

'You dare to threaten me?'

'Tomorrow I will tell the authorities. With my connections in this city—you see, I am a true Roman and you are not—they will arrest you as a sodomite. They will surely be interested to hear that you live with a fourteen-year-old boy. While you are burning at the stake, I will be lying with Fillide. We will celebrate your sorry end with a good, hard fuck.'

Michele spits out, 'You dare to bite your thumb at me!? I should poke out your eyes and leave your corpse for the rats.'

Michele takes a deep breath, controls himself and walks on, continuing down the street toward his dwelling, shaking off Tomassoni's threats. But as he passes by his enemy, their eyes meet and the hot coal in Michele's brain explodes. In an instant, Michele's rapier is in hand. With one hard thrust, before the other can pull his weapon all the way out, he drives his sword into Tomassoni's throat, out the back of his neck and into the wall, pinning him against it. Tomassoni struggles and gags, his windpipe severed, blood dribbling from his mouth. Silenced, he stares in shock.

When Michele pulls out his sword, the blood gushes like water bubbling from a fountain. He watches as Tomassoni slumps to the ground, dead. As Michele stares down, amazed at the swiftness of his own violence, three young men come blundering down the alley, drunk. One of them, suddenly sober, asks, 'What happened here? Are you not Signor Michelangelo Merisi, the artist?'

Michele glances at them, says nothing in reply, and walks away.

He does not hurry or run, and the drunks don't follow him. At first, he feels nothing. Strangely, he imagines the light reflecting from the armour of the soldiers come to arrest him by lamplight. Then another thought intrudes. *Tomassoni has four brothers, all soldiers. I cannot remain in Rome.*

———————

Michele hurries into his studio. 'Cecco! Cecco!'

The boy appears. 'What is it? What is wrong?'

'We must leave. Now!'

'Leave? What do you mean? Why?'

Michele starts throwing a few necessities into a sack and looks at the boy. 'I have killed Ranuccio Tomassoni. I didn't mean to, it just happened. Quickly now.'

The look on the boy's face is an odd combination of shock and willing obedience.

Minutes later, they go to the door and glance out. The street is deserted. Less than an hour has passed since the death of Ranuccio.

They hurry through the dark streets and alleys to Palazzo Madama, the shadows at their feet shifting and creeping among the cobbles with a lugubrious weight.

'Who goes there?' The guard at the gate stops them and holds up a lamp to see their faces. 'Ah, His Eminence's artist.'

'I must see the cardinal immediately. It is an emergency.' He notices the iron grilles on the ground-floor windows around the courtyard, resembling a prison.

'Too late,' insists the guard. 'His Eminence has surely gone to bed.'

Michele leans into the gateway and looks up to the second storey above the courtyard, the *piano nobile* of the palazzo. 'No, there is a light in his rooms. I absolutely must see him now. If the cardinal learns that you have delayed me, he will have your head.'

The guard glances up to the illuminated window. He hesitates. 'Very well. Come.'

He speaks to a servant inside who disappears and returns shortly. This servant motions for Michele to follow him to Del Monte's study. 'Cecco, wait here until I return.'

As Michele enters, he recognizes something new in the room, the large clock on a side table. 'My apologies if I awoke you, Your Eminence.' Del Monte sits in his throne-like chair, a book open in his hands.

'No, no, I was not asleep. But an intrusion at this hour ... What is it? You look disturbed, my son.'

On an impulse, Michele steps forward, takes the cardinal's hand and kisses his ring. This is a ritual they have dispensed with over the years as their relationship grew less formal.

The cardinal raises his eyebrows as Michele steps back. 'What is on your mind?'

Michele changes the story to make it appear more in the nature of self-defence than it in fact was. 'I did not mean to kill him,' Michele insists. 'He attacked me. It was an accident ... an accident.' This is not entirely untrue, for if Michele took time to think it over, he knows he would have preferred to injure or maim Ranuccio. Killing him will bring down the heavy hand of the law and the revenge of the Tomassoni family on his head. *If only I had taken time to think. Killing him was not worth banishment from Rome.* 'I have an uncontrollable temper, Your Eminence, as you know. My greatest fault.'

Del Monte nods. 'Yes, I know. It remains a problem for you. But I believe you when you say it was an accident. I have considered myself your protector for a number of years and I will not abandon you now. I will go to tell my servant to order the *maestro di stalla* to ready a carriage to take you away from the city. You will be travelling under my protection. Wait here until I return to hear your confession and give you forgiveness. The rest is in God's hands.'

As the cardinal hurries from the room to find his servant, Michele notices again the clock on the side table near the door. He eyes it closely. *That is the Frenchman's clock whose gears bit me.*

An hour later, Michele and Cecco bump along in one of the cardinal's carriages, well beyond the walls of Rome, heading southwest past tiny, sleeping villages, and rolling through the countryside. The moon, near to full, silvers the fields, and the stars are gathered in clusters.

Michele stares out at the passing landscape. *Michelangelo Buonarotti, my namesake, too had to flee Rome, afraid that the architect Bramante was preparing to have him murdered.*

'What are you thinking?' Cecco asks.

'Nothing of importance.' Michele leans his head back and closes his eyes. 'I wonder if all my painting now will have to be done in the style of Mantegna's famous vault in Mantua.'

'Remind me,' Cecco says. 'How did Mantegna paint that high ceiling?'

'He painted the figures as if they were staring down from a cupola above. The style is called *di sotto in su*, "from below upwards".'

---

Early the next morning the carriage arrives at the gates of a hill-top fortress on the edge of a small town. Before the carriage even comes to a full stop, a servant seated next to the driver leaps down and presents a letter to the guard.

'For Duke Marzio Colonna from His Eminence, Cardinal Francesco Del Monte.'

As they step down from the carriage, Michele looks up and asks the driver, 'What is this place called?'

'Paliano,' he replies. 'We are southwest of Rome.'

Michele notices that the surrounding fields and vineyards in the distance are shining with dew, and the birds of late spring send up a chorus of song, marking another day as if nothing in the world has changed. Michele has met the duke, a long-time friend of the cardinal's, several times previously at Palazzo Madama during feasts but can recall little about the man. One key fact he does remember is that another member of the Colonnas lived in the village of Caravaggio and was a long-time patron of Michele's family.

One of the duke's servants emerges a short while later and addresses Michele and Cecco. 'His Excellency will see you later this morning. You will have a room in which to make yourselves comfortable and have a rest. Don Colonna wishes to assure you that any friend of the cardinal's is a friend of his. Come.'

The next day, after meeting the duke and settling in, Michele requests a room which he and Cecco can use as a studio. 'Also, is there an apothecary in the town? We will need pigments and canvas.' A short while later, a servant returns. 'I will purchase whatever you require. His Excellency says you are not to show your face in the town, according to the wishes of the cardinal.'

Two days later, Michele and Cecco have all the materials they need to begin. Michele immediately throws himself back into his work, trying to shed the events of the previous few days. He feels as if his past has been chopped off and fallen away into an abyss.

# ⋅⊰ THE ASSASSIN ⊱⋅

---

I head across Piazza Navona in the late afternoon under a low grey sky. As I have no money, I cannot even enter a tavern. I hope I will find someone to give me work. Perhaps I can model tomorrow for the painter, or maybe I can offer my services to another artist. I could mention I have experience as a model. The Jews, as usual, are out selling used clothes. I could wait until later, when they leave, and rob one of them again in a back alley. I wouldn't get much, but it would be something. I hear my stomach rumbling.

Just then, off in the distance, I spot Carlo the Ear scanning the crowd. I approach and he sees me. 'Ah, Luca, I've been looking for you. Let us go somewhere we can talk.'

We leave the piazza and saunter down one of the nearby streets, heads leaning together as he tells me he has work.

I try to hide my pleasure at this news, but I nearly burst into tears of relief. It must be the hunger. I manage to control myself. 'What is it?'

'You have heard that the younger Tomassoni, Ranuccio, was murdered last night?'

'This news had not reached my ears, but, it is no great loss.'

'Do you know who murdered him?'

'It wasn't me, if that's what you mean.'

'No, no. I know it wasn't you. They say it was that artist you have been working for. Michelangelo Merisi. He was spotted at the scene and the authorities are looking for him.'

I immediately sense the opportunity. 'Who wants to hire me, the dead man's family?'

'Before I say, you agree to give me half of whatever they pay you? For finding you the job, you understand.'

'Damn, but you are a thief. I have to admit I am desperate for work, though I should not be telling you that. Half it is.'

'Good. Then it is settled. Tomassoni has four brothers, all soldiers. They want to hire an assassin, to find the artist and kill him.'

'Why do they not do it themselves?'

'This Michelangelo Merisi might be difficult to find. He has wealthy and powerful friends and he appears to have fled Rome. The usual story, yes? But the Tomassonis want him dead. Ranuccio was the youngest son. Everyone is asking how he, a soldier and a talented swordsman, could have lost a fight with an artist. His reputation is in ruins. The family honour is sullied. They will pay well to restore it.'

'How well?'

'Five hundred scudi,' says Carlo.

'So little? Are you sure you're being honest with me, my friend?'

'It is a fair offer. Half for you, half for me. You can count on them to pay. And, as I understand it, Luca, you are in no position to bargain. You will not be rich as a Medici, but, I repeat, it is a good offer.'

I rub my chin. Yes, it's work I need, but I do not trust Carlo the Ear. He would steal coins off the eyes of a dead man. The family likely offered much more than the five hundred scudi he admitted to me. 'I want to talk to them.'

Carlo is suddenly nervous. 'Not necessary. They said I could hire someone to do the job. They will pay. You don't want them to know who is doing their dirty work for them. That would not be wise.'

'I want to meet with them. Their street isn't far. I know it.' I begin walking in that direction without looking back. Carlo, resigned, hurries behind.

───────────

Alessandro Tomassoni, the eldest, speaks for the rest of the family. I have seen him around; that is how I know his name. He is in his mid-thirties, wide-shouldered, with a broad, lined face, as if he has seen many years of war and pain. 'He was our youngest brother. A young lion with a great future ahead of him. This *cazzo* artist will pay. We want you to hunt him down and kill him like a dog in the street.'

The other three brothers sitting around the room nod their heads. They all wear their swords.

I listen, say nothing. Patience is my strong suit. When I am on the hunt for a victim, I can wait for days, months, even years if necessary. I know the situation will eventually ripen. For now I will let things take their course.

As I do not respond, Alessandro continues. 'Carlo says you have experience in this sort of thing, as an assassin, that is.'

'Yes.' I say no more. I want them to understand that an assassin is different from a soldier. An assassin must be a shadow, able to disappear in a moment. To strike, like lightning from a clear blue sky, when least expected. Timing. An assassin must be a master of timing.

One of the other brothers speaks up, the one with an unruly beard. 'What are we to make of your silence? How will you find this Merisi and kill him? Tell us. Now.'

'I will find him, I will become his shadow, and I will kill him. That is all you need to know.'

He nods his head, considering my response. I sense they begin to appreciate my near wordless confidence.

Another younger brother asks, 'You will bring us back his head as proof?'

'No. I do not travel around with heads in my sack. You will know that he is dead, have no fear.'

The oldest brother, Alessandro, speaks again. 'Carlo told you what we are offering as payment?'

'No, he said nothing.'

Carlo's face drops but before he can spurt out a word of denial, Alessandro says, 'Eight hundred scudi. It is a good offer. We want him dead. You accept?'

'Yes.' I look at Carlo who refuses to meet my gaze. 'Of the total, two hundred to Carlo and the rest to me. You'll give me four hundred now, and the rest when you have been assured that he is dead. Agreed?'

Carlo leans forward to argue but sees the brothers solemnly nod their heads in agreement, so he keeps silent.

'One last thing,' I add before leaving. 'You will never know my name, and if Carlo reports me to the police or tries to make me pay for his silence, you will agree to slit his throat and throw his lifeless body in the Tiber.'

'Agreed,' Alessandro says grimly and I take my leave.

## ⊰ THE ARTIST ⊱

Within a week, word comes from Cardinal Del Monte that the Papal authorities have passed a sentence of death on Michele. The cardinal explains in a letter, addressed to the duke and given to Michele, that he can do nothing for the time being to change the sentence. But a cardinal, as Michele knows, has many high-level contacts, people of standing he can call on for favours. Del Monte will continue to work on obtaining a pardon for Michele's crimes. Michele allows himself faint hope for an eventual return.

Meanwhile, Michele immerses himself in a daily regimen of painting, working like a demon with its hair on fire to forget his difficult situation. Cecco too continues his apprenticeship with Michele and works hard at it, but not obsessively like the older artist. Michele feels he will fall into a deep well of oblivion if he even goes a single day without working at his art.

Michele begins work on a painting of Mary Magdalen in ecstasy. His image of Magdalen is drawn from his memory of his lover, Fillide.

Since he has no models here, he must try to recall every detail of Fillide's face and form. The memory of those images burns in his heart, setting him aflame and leaving him scorched. His longing for Fillide is painful, and their future together is now in doubt. He stops, steps back, stares at the painting. Shakes his head. It is a dark, brooding work with a nearly black background, fitting his mood.

'Is something wrong?' Cecco asks him from across the room. He has been working on his own painting, a basket of white carnations. 'You do not like your picture?'

'It is too dark.'

'Lighten it,' Cecco suggests.

Michele shakes his head again. He is disturbed that he cannot seem to escape his sense of gloom and that his state of mind is finding its way into his paintings. He does not want to admit to young Cecco, so innocent in the ways of love, the reason for his sorrow.

No news comes from Rome. The summer grows unbearably hot and uncomfortable in the fortress at Paliano, which feels to Michele like a prison. He never shows his face in the town as he fears he will be recognized and turned over to the Tomassoni family or the authorities. He realizes that a well-known face is one of the disadvantages of fame. He keeps busy, working in the studio provided him by the duke and wandering with Cecco about the forests and vineyards of the nearby estate.

In the fall, word comes of possible future commissions in Naples, arranged by the duke. Michele is surprised. He wonders if they haven't heard that he killed a man, or whether his reputation as an artist outweighs that consideration. In any case, he is pleased. The duke is heading to Naples to spend the winter months. He can provide Michele safe passage in his own carriage, accompanied by a small company of the duke's private soldiers. The duke explains that the Tomassonis will surely be watching for him along the principal routes between Rome and other major cities. The soldiers are a necessity.

Cecco meanwhile decides he will not accompany Michele on this next portion of his journey. He will return to Lombardy, his apprenticeship concluded. Michele tells Cecco that he is sorry to see him go. *Another part of my life falling away.*

Michele wonders if he should send for Fillide. He longs for her companionship and wants her to accompany him to Naples. As he is about to request a messenger to send to Rome, it strikes him how foolish this would be. Fillide, without knowing it, could lead the Tomassoni family directly to him. In his frustration, he throws a pot of scarlet paint at the wall. It explodes and runs down in deep red streaks.

## ◄{ THE ASSASSIN }►

---

I realize that damned artist could be hiding anywhere. He could still be in the city, or he might have fled. He has connections with high-level clergy, such as Cardinal Del Monte and Cardinal Mattei. Any of his wealthy private patrons, Guistiniani the banker or the Contarelli family, could be hiding him in one of their vast palazzos in Rome or on one of their country estates.

It was easy enough for me to discover the names of the painter's supporters. It is common knowledge in certain circles. At the tavernas where the artists gather, everyone speaks openly about him, both friends of his and enemies. Even Carlo the Ear is able to add some information, now that he has overcome his foolish anger with me. But still, I hope for a breakthrough when I arrive at Cardinal Del Monte's Palazzo Madama and pass the groom there a few small coins.

'Perhaps you could answer a few questions for me.' I watch as the groom eagerly shoves the coins into his pocket. The tousle-haired young servant looks as messy as a pile of straw, as if he sleeps in his clothes with the horses. It is now four days since the murder.

The groom shrugs his shoulders and tugs at his short, scruffy beard. 'Perhaps.'

'Did you notice anything unusual the night of May 29 around the palazzo?'

'May 29? What day was that?'

'It was the night of the murder of Ranuccio Tomassoni by Michelangelo Merisi, the artist who once lived here. The cardinal was his patron. Have you heard about the murder?'

'Of course. The whole city knows.'

'Was there any unusual activity here that night?'

The groom reflects a moment, staring down at his feet. 'The only thing I recall is that His Eminence's *maestro di stalla* came to me late and ordered that I hitch the horses to one of the carriages. The carriage left the palazzo shortly thereafter.'

'Was that unusual?'

'Not so unusual, but the cardinal was here in the palazzo the next morning—I saw him standing at his window.' He points to a window on the second level.

'And?'

'The carriage had not returned.'

———————

The next day I go to see the painter's landlady.

'I have not seen him in days,' she says, 'and he owes me rent.'

'Did he tell you where he was going?'

'No. Not a word. He just took off like a bird. Left everything behind, as far as I can tell.'

'Everything?'

'Yes. His painting supplies are still in his studio, as well as a canvas, a half-finished painting, his pigments. I don't know what to do with his possessions. Are you a friend of his?'

'No, no, not at all.'

She gives me a quizzical look and I leave. I know now what my next step will be.

---

For two months, I have been searching for Merisi in the towns and estates surrounding the city of Rome. I know he left the city and so many of his friends and patrons have country estates where he could be hiding. Everywhere I go, I ask questions, of servants, of grooms, of townspeople. Of course, I cannot get close to the wealthy landowners, but the servants always know many intimate details of life on these estates. Still, nothing. It is as if Merisi has become a ghost, has disappeared like fading mist.

As I ride, I think again how I have come to appreciate this fine horse the Tomassonis have loaned me. They were hesitant about it at first, but I told them the artist had left the city and that I could not hope to find him without a horse to travel about the countryside in search of him.

I tick off the villages and towns I have visited in the past months, through the heat of the summer. I suspect—no, I know—that Merisi cannot have gone far from Rome, for the carriage that spirited him away was back in place at Palazzo Madama the next day. How far can a carriage travel in one night? Although, of course, he may have already moved on.

First, I set out for Ostia, the port near Rome, stopping in villages with posting inns along the way to feed and water the horse as necessary. I reason that perhaps Merisi headed by ship to Genoa or Naples, or even Sicily. By the docks, I encounter an old man sitting in the shade looking out at the water with his tired eyes. Every port has its ancient salt who watches and marks everyone who passes, noticing anything out of the ordinary. Certainly, a cardinal's carriage from Rome would have been remarkable in Ostia. But the old man has seen nothing.

Since then, I have been visiting all the towns and villages in a circle about Rome, those that are within a one-night's carriage ride. I slink about the estates, palazzos and fortresses that belong to families of those connected to the artist, hoping to catch a glimpse of him. I pay out coins to the guards and servants, buying information—and their silence. I have a simple plan. When I am on the hunt for prey, I feel most alive.

After Ostia, I head for Castel Gandolfo, the pope's summer residence overlooking Lake Albano, southeast of Rome. As I ride, I keep my eye out for bands of brigands. These desperate, starving men would surely slice me ear to ear for my horse and my small bag of coins. Most of the large payment from the Tomassonis is well hidden in Rome. Luckily, I am able to avoid any untoward confrontations on the road.

In Castel Gandolfo, I stop a Franciscan priest wearing robes and a wide black hat walking along the street of the town. I describe the carriage and the artist.

He shakes his head. 'I have seen no one of that description.'

From there I make my way to the town of Frascati. I arrive late in the day and spend the evening in a taverna's courtyard drinking their famous white wine, which goes down like rainwater. I have been on the road for over a month, baking every day in the sun, my skin dry and cracked and burnt brown, and I am sick of it.

Though the wine is delicious and refreshing, it delivers a gouging hangover like no other. I am in my element the next day, stopping every twenty minutes to slide down from the horse and vomit in the dust. No one in Frascati had seen the famous artist, though the place is thick with eight or ten villas, any one of which could be hiding him.

Next, I pass through the Sabine Hills to Tivoli. No sign of the artist. Then along the River Ariene with its waterfalls, rather thin at this time of year but still useful for watering the horse and myself.

I ride on. Up and down steep hills, through deep ravines,

mounting to hilltop villages, across fields dusty with the end of summer. In the villages that are too small to boast an apothecary's shop selling artist pigments, I make quick stops to inquire about the artist, but soon ride on. In larger towns that do boast a shop, I enter and inquire if they have had a request in the past several months for a large supply of pigments and other painting supplies. I know, without a doubt, that the artist will continue to work wherever he is.

As his model, I had witnessed his obsession. He must paint, every day, constantly. He lives for nothing else. And the landlady said he took no painting supplies with him.

Several of the apothecaries note that they had received recent requests for pigments and artist supplies from local artists. None of these orders, however, has been delivered to a local estate or villa.

I am sitting in a small taverna in a town near Tivoli, saddle-sore and half-drunk, when a rider from the Tomassonis finds me.

'I have been looking for you for days,' the rider says. 'The brothers grow impatient. Have you found him?'

'Tell them that great patience is required for this job. I will find the artist and I will kill him, but it will take the time it takes. Tell them to let me do my work. I have not run off with their payment, have I? I am making good progress. I have a plan.'

'What plan?'

'That is none of their business. I will fulfill my obligation.'

I turn to the innkeeper. 'What is the next town east of here?'

'Paliano,' he replies from the far side of the room.

'I will go there next,' I inform the rider. 'Tell the Tomassonis I will not give up until I find him and kill him.'

The next day I head to another town instead, to the north. I do not want the Tomassoni brothers haunting my footsteps.

I finally arrive in Paliano ten days later and discover that this town is home to a fortress belonging to Duke Colonna, a friend of Cardinal Del Monte. A few small coins later (rural servants and gate guards come cheaper than those in the city), I learn that 'the artist' staying in the fortress left a week ago.

'Where did he go?'

'The master goes to Naples at this time of year, for several months. I believe the artist was with him. Not the younger one, though. He went home to Lombardy.'

*Perhaps I'm not as good a hunter as I thought. I will return to Rome and inform the brothers that I will now follow Merisi to Naples.*


## ⚜ THE ARTIST ⚜

---

'You have been to Naples?'

'Never.' Michele notes that the duke has the face of a meat cleaver—all parts pointed, led by the nose. His eyebrows are peaked like triangles, his mouth somewhat angular, his ears slightly pointed.

'My apologies for not meeting since your arrival at Paliano. I have had to travel back to Rome several times and have been extremely busy. By your accent, I surmise you are from the north, yes?'

'It is true. Near Milan. A village called Caravaggio. A member of the Colonna family was the Marchese in our village. Perhaps a relative of yours?'

'A distant cousin. Your family were farmers? Or perhaps merchants?'

'Farmers. I was raised by my uncle after my father and mother died. I apprenticed to a painter in Milan.'

Duke Marzio Colonna sits opposite Michele in the carriage as it rattles down the hill of Paliano. The morning sun is just cresting the horizon as they set out on the long journey to Naples.

Four of the duke's well-armed soldiers ride along with them, two on each side.

'Tell me.' The duke tilts his head. 'Are you not a member of the Academy of Saint Luke, like many of the better Roman artists? I hear that the Academy is allowed to pardon one condemned man each year on the feast of Saint Luke, patron saint of painters. You should take advantage of this if you have friends in the Academy willing to help.'

Michele turns away from the passing fields to regard the duke. 'Your Excellency, I have no friends in the Academy. In fact, the members have been the butt of my slurs and insults for years. They are not genuine artists. Fakes and sycophants all. I will look for no support from that quarter and, moreover, I expect none.'

'What about His Eminence Cardinal Del Monte or the pope himself? Did not one of the popes many years ago intervene on behalf of the artist Benvenuto Cellini, absolving him of several murders? In fact, I have heard that Pope Paul III once said that artists like Cellini should not be subject to the law. But our present pope clearly has other views.'

'His Eminence the Cardinal has told me he is working on it. We will see.' Michele changes the subject. 'Will your wife and children stay in Paliano?'

'No, they will come later, in a few days. I have business to attend to in Naples and must arrive there as soon as possible.'

'I see. What can you tell me about the city? You know it well?'

'Yes, I do. I spend some months there every year. It is a place quite different than Rome. The presence of the Spanish is troublesome, of course. Spanish soldiers garrison there, which causes endless tension and trouble with the Neapolitans. Constant fights in taverns and such. As much the fault of the Neapolitans as the Spaniards, believe me. The feeling of hatred is mutual.'

'Is it as large as Rome?'

'At least three times the size. You must understand, the city lives forever on the edge of revolt. Revolt is in the Neapolitan nature. You have heard of Giordano Bruno, the heretic burned in 1600?'

'Yes. I was there in the campo to witness it.'

'Bruno was from Naples. It tells you something about the stubbornness of the people.'

Michele pauses a moment, then asks 'Are there numerous artists in the city?'

'Not as in Rome. Fewer private collectors. Plentiful churches, of course, and church commissions, but the clergy in Naples, despite Bruno, tend to be arch-conservative. But be assured, your reputation as an artist has spread to Naples. You will have no trouble finding work there. I will make inquiries on your behalf.'

'I appreciate your efforts, Your Excellency. What else can you tell me about the place?'

'Naples is surrounded by beauty: the sea sparkles blue, Vesuvius hisses and belches occasionally but does no serious harm. The nearby islands and coastlines are lovely, the air smelling of lemons in season, but the city feels far different from Rome. While it boasts handsome palazzos near the sea, Naples itself is crowded, or perhaps I should say, overcrowded. The dwellings in the poor areas tower five six seven storeys into the sky, making the streets narrow and dark. Sometimes it seems as if the buildings are leaning, about to fall into each other. Naples does not breathe like Rome. It is a city that has the best and the worst of everything.'

For a while, Michele enjoys this tutoring on the city of Naples. He is glad that the duke is talkative and knowledgeable and yet something unctuous about the duke puts Michele off. Too smooth, too oily.

'It is a wealthy city, but also a filthy and depraved one. You can find anything you want in Naples. As I said, the best and the worst.' The duke leans his head back and closes his eyes.

Michele gazes out the window at the passing fields, hills with vineyards in the distance. At that moment, the image of Fillide comes to him. He dwells for a while on those pleasant, sensuous memories.

'Something else you should know,' the duke says, waking with a start as if he had never stopped talking. 'Naples is a dangerous city.

Once we arrive, you will stay in my palazzo where I can provide you living arrangements and a decent-sized studio for you to work in.'

'My gratitude is profound, Your Excellency.'

'Over the years, Cardinal Del Monte has provided many favours to me and my family. His request that I become your guardian in this difficult time for you is the least I can do in return. When we arrive in Naples, I have a man there, a trusted servant, one of the best swordsmen in the realm. Guido will be your personal guard and will accompany you wherever you go.'

'That is not necessary.' The idea of being dogged by this loyal manservant feels instantly like a burden.

'You have no choice. The cardinal has asked that I ensure your safety. I have given my word that I would.'

'I doubt that the Tomassoni brothers will bother troubling themselves to trace me to Naples.'

'It is not the Tomassonis I worry about; though, if I were you, I would be careful not to underestimate their desire for vengeance. No, it is not the brothers who are your great danger in Naples. It is the Neapolitans.'

'Your Excellency, I have my rapier, and I know how to use it.'

———

On his first full day in Naples, Michele sneaks out of the palazzo before he can be assigned his guard. The carriage arrived the night before in the dark, so he saw little of the city on the way in. Now he wants to wander and discover for himself where he has landed.

The duke's palazzo stands near the seafront, which is lined with other grand palaces and official buildings. It is fronted by palm trees and looks out at the blue Mediterranean and the great arc of the Bay of Naples, with Vesuvius looming in the distance to the south. Unmoved by the great beauty before him, Michele turns away from the view and heads into the city.

After a short walk, the wide boulevard gives way to a maze of narrow streets, crowded with locals going about their business. Little light penetrates to the depths of the lanes; the tall, narrow buildings have shallow balconies that almost touch each other overhead. Everywhere, heaps of garbage: rotting fruit, fish bones, one pile of refuse with a goat head on top, eyeless but still seeming to stare at him. In that heap, three young children, perhaps six or seven years of age, dressed in scraps and rags, dig through the rot looking for anything edible.

Every ten steps the smell of human excrement assaults him. There's a man urinating against a wall, a pair of dogs rutting in the street, a runnel of fetid water stagnating in the middle of the lane. The smells nearly gag him: putrid meat, human sweat from the passing crowds, the stench of a nearby tannery.

He looks up. The sky is a thin line high above, between the buildings. Naples is far more claustrophobic than Rome, its poor areas poorer, its piazzas smaller, its churches meaner. Every square offers as sentinel its impassive, dark church with little architectural interest.

Ahead Michele spots an opening into a piazza and hurries for it to try to escape the nightmare stench of the narrow alley. As he strides into the square, he notes that the air clears slightly. Across the way, a dozen swarthy beggars block the entrance to the church. A woman dressed in torn robes holds an infant so quiet and still that he would swear it is dead. The outside of the church is decorated with poorly-executed sculptures of saints and martyrs, almost sickening in their overdone detail. A number of Spanish soldiers stand about in small groups on the piazza, talking and looking askance and with suspicion at the Neapolitans.

A few of the soldiers watch as two men, wearing red tights and puffed sleeves, box barehanded, employing a sparring form called *civettino*, in which one man holds the other in place by pressing his foot on top of the other's. Near an alley, a peasant plays a small bagpipe; in another corner of the square, three girls dance a quick, manic *saltarello*.

Watching them, a matron nurses a puppy from her own breast. A throbbing, dissolute energy infects the place like a plague.

Down one wider street he can see Vesuvius looming in the distance, exerting a powerful influence on the city, as if death were close and could arrive in an instant. Up out of the earth and down from the sky.

Michele realizes that a small crowd of five or six young men across the square has noticed him. Menacingly, they move toward him, an obvious non-local, his fine garments marking him as a potentially lucrative target. He spins about and hurries down a nearby alley while the gang breaks into a run. Michele slips into a tavern, goes to the bar, and orders a pot of wine. Some unwritten rule, his instincts tell him, will keep the crowd of young toughs from entering the bar. As the first of them is about to enter at the door, the tavern keeper, a burly man, glances up. He shouts to the back room and instantly two more strong-looking men appear. The toughs see this and soon disperse. Michele stays until night has fallen, then hurries back through unlit streets to the duke's palazzo.

The next morning, the guard assigned by the duke comes to Michele in his studio. He is a large man, tall and wide, as expected, with a huge square head seemingly cut from granite or marble. 'I am Guido, your protector,' he says simply. Michele nods and continues setting out his paints and brushes. Guido sits down on a chair and watches in silence.

Michele rather likes Guido on first meeting. He senses the guard will prove a good drinking companion and will be someone with whom he can explore the city. Michele instinctively knows that any dust-ups with roustabouts on the streets or drunken revels with whores will never reach the ears of the duke or the cardinal.

Within several days, Michele's studio is ready and he sets to work on a private commission. The work had been ordered by a wealthy ship owner who instructed the artist to include 'choirs of angels' in the painting according to his wife's wishes. Michele ends up painting as his own passions dictate—no choirs of angels ever appear. After a moment's hesitation on viewing the painting, the wife and her uxorious husband are reasonably satisfied. Michele is spared the need to bow to bad taste to earn his keep, and the payment proves generous.

Soon, a second substantial commission comes his way. A charitable institution orders a large painting depicting the Seven Mercies for the main altar of their church. Naples is swarming with these religious groups trying to ease the suffering and save the souls of the poor. When Michele speaks to the two pious gentlemen from the Pio Monte della Misericordia to negotiate the terms of the work, they offer a huge sum—four hundred ducats—for the painting.

It is an enormous painting—thirteen feet high by nine feet wide. He throws himself into the work and for weeks on end forgets all about the Tomassonis and his previous life, save for the occasional painful memory of Fillide. Rather than dwelling on thoughts of who might be with her now, he lives inside the painting, day and night.

At one point, he has a momentary insight. *Only a demon could have such vigour, only a creature blind with creativity and ambition could have this drive. One has to be running from the fires of hell to labour like this.* He becomes lost in another realm while he works on the painting. Nothing can touch him. He is moving too fast through the world, through the ether, through the heavens, and through hell too. The flames cannot touch him. He is too alive, too driven. He himself is on fire. *Fire cannot burn fire. As long as I am working, I am free.*

Trailed by Guido, he hurries down the streets of Naples for inspiration. He refuses to view the tired paintings of religious history that cover the walls of the city's churches. His is a crowded painting, like the streets themselves—a teeming nightmare, a frenzied opera of angels and saints and soldiers and victims and, to one side, a beautiful young woman suckling a bearded old prisoner with her plump breast,

while drops of her milk dot his beard. Will they allow it? He never hesitates, continues to work. He will paint what he will paint.

Although he titles it *The Seven Works of Mercy*, it would be difficult to find anything religious about it. It's a scene ripped from the roiling, stinking streets of Naples. He paints the crippled, the thirsty, the starving, the dead, the naked, the sick. A painting of nightmare theatre. His hallucination. His delirium. His fever dream of madness.

He seldom eats, works through the night by lamplight. Once or twice a day, he throws down his brush and rushes outside for inspiration. Wide-eyed, he hurries through the streets, winding through the crowds, Giudo close on his tail. Michele works in a mania of effort, exertion, and obsession. He convinces himself that he has to believe, beyond any hope or reason, that he will become a great painter, his reputation exploding and spreading far and wide to such an extent that, in the end, Rome will have no choice but to take him back.

---

From this point, the rest of Michele's life is about running—running away and running to. Away from those hunting him, away from the Tomassoni brothers, away from Rome and back to Rome, running away from the unknown, while running toward his future, toward Fillide, toward his patrons in Rome and greater fame, and his date with destiny.

When running *away* and running *to* become perfectly balanced, one arrives at a final still point and the world stops.

# ⊰ THE ASSASSIN ⊱

---

After hastening to Rome to apprise the Tomassonis of my movements and assure them of my continued commitment, I board a boat to Naples, intent on killing the artist as promised. Alessandro Tomassoni indicated that the family was growing impatient with my lack of progress, and after months of travel, I was more anxious than ever to fulfill my commission and collect the remaining payment.

I detest this city, with that damned volcano looming. I have been to Naples before, on another job, one that worked out well. A fashionable young man who refused to hide his face in public and took foolish chances in dark alleys. I hope this one works out as well. But it will not be easy. It seldom is.

I have learned not to trust these Neapolitans. One moment they are joking and laughing, the next you are apt to discover that all their humour is mockery, and the moment after that they are attempting to slit your throat.

On arrival in Naples, I start seeking out a tavern, the kind of establishment where information of the kind I need finds its way. Every city has such a tavern and its own 'Carlo the Ear' installed within, and I suspect Naples has more than one. And I am right. I find an informant named Aldo on my second day.

For a reasonable sum, I learn that Duke Colonna, who owns a large palazzo on the waterfront, has arrived back in the city with a guest. An artist from Rome rumoured to be wanted there for murder. But my local informant provides a bit of extra information for free.

The man is not old but looks worn out by hard living. He lowers his head near the end of our meeting and says, 'You have heard of Colonna's man, the head of his guards?'

'No. Why would I?'

'I am sure his fame has spread as far as Rome. This man is named Guido and he remains fiercely loyal to Don Colonna. Do not ever engage this man in swordplay. You will lose your hands first, and then your head. He is an expert with rapier and stiletto. At all costs, avoid this Guido. Your life may depend on it.'

The man goes on to describe Guido for me. The square head, the freakishly long arms. He will be easy to spot when the time comes.

And the time is not long in coming.

Two nights later, I hide in a nearby alley while I wait and watch outside Duke Colonna's palazzo. I see the artist exit and hurry down the street. He looks obsessed, his eyes wide, his mind engaged elsewhere. Good, this should be simple. My hand goes to the hilt of my sword.

Then I notice, bounding out of the building behind him, a man who must be this Guido about whom I have been warned. The artist turns and speaks to him. I am not close enough to hear what he says, but I see that Guido nods, and walks behind as the artist strides on. I follow at a safe distance.

They proceed along the streets, turning here and there, walking a long while until they come to one of the gloomiest quarters of the city. But this Guido never leaves off. He appears light-footed but tight with tension, as if his body is the tough, twisted trunk of an olive tree.

I decide not to engage. I will wait. I cannot let pressure from the Tomassonis force me to make a false move. There is always a right time, that moment when two fates come together, and only one leaves.

———————

For weeks on end, it continues like this. I wait outside the palazzo. Some evenings the artist comes out, and on others he never appears. He never takes a step without his guard behind him or beside him. This Guido is as observant as the artist is blind. Merisi walks through the city lost in thought, probably churning up pictures and paintings in his imagination, while his guard has his eyes open in every direction. The man is nothing but eyes that watch and see everything. He never stops to talk to anyone, never loses sight of Merisi.

When the two of them pass through a crowded street or square, Guido follows closely behind the artist. In a pinch, he could reach around him with those long arms and stick his rapier into an attacker in front of them.

One time, a young woman comes too near, perhaps to offer her services. By the time Merisi glances up, Guido has forcefully pushed her away. She stumbles into a wall, rights herself and hurries away.

But it gives me an idea. Merisi loves his whores and cannot do without one for long. Several times, the artist and his guard have entered houses that I know are bordellos. I can't imagine that he allows the guard into the room with him and his chosen whore. There, perhaps, exists an opening for me, a crack.

———————

Early evening and the sun sets over the nearby Bay of Naples while I wait to see if the artist will appear with Guido. I can taste the salty mist of the sea on my lips. As I stare out at the water burnished with sunset, I wonder where to get food and drink this evening—and I nearly miss the appearance of Merisi. He and the guard have exited the palazzo and are sauntering along together far down the street. The artist appears to no longer resist the presence of Guido. They are not chatting, but strolling companionably. The guard projects his usual awareness of the surroundings. Again, I follow at a safe distance.

When they come to a thickly populated section of the city, Merisi stops and talks to Guido, who nods. They enter a nearby doorway. I approach and a shiver of excitement passes through me. I let it go. Excitement proves deadly in my work.

I enter through the same doorway and discover it's a brothel, as I

guessed. The artist and his guard are just disappearing up the stairs with a young prostitute. I had hoped Guido might wait in the sitting room, but in this I have no luck. The madam approaches me and I request a girl. I barely glance at her before heading up the stairs behind her.

Upstairs, she leads me into a long hallway lined with doors, all closed. Outside one of the doors down the hall, Guido sits on a chair. Luckily the girl shows me to the nearest room and we enter. I have taken care to keep my head bowed and my back to Guido so the guard never glimpses my face.

In the room, the window is boarded over. I assume that the same is true in all the rooms. My disappointment is momentary. It will prove impossible to enter the artist's room from the hall, due to the presence of his guard, and entry from the window will also clearly be impossible. I let it go. Perhaps tomorrow my chance will come. At some point—it always happens, with the inevitability of a clock's hand turning—they will let down their guard. I have my way with the girl, in a bed filthy and flea-ridden, barely looking at her. I pay and leave.

# ⊰ THE ARTIST ⊱

---

Michele works in his new studio, using a painter's mahl-stick to steady his brush. The ursine Guido, arms dangling well past his knees, sits watching. Like Vesuvius, Guido is solid and still, but ready to erupt into action at any moment. Turning slightly, he glances at the door which he keeps in the corner of his eye at all times.

Michele works in a frenzy of activity, feeling that if he just keeps painting great works of art, he will be forgiven his sins and be called back to Rome. And, by staying extremely busy his mind will not be tortured by his desire to return to his previous life.

Guido clears his throat. 'A moment, please, master. There is something we must discuss.'

Michele ignores him for several moments, his back to the guard while he finishes a few strokes on the gnarled, ugly foot he is painting. He pauses, wipes his brush with a cloth, stabs it into a pot filled with other brushes. He leans back against the table. 'Yes?'

'Perhaps you would like to sit?'

'No. I am too agitated. What is so important you must interrupt my work?'

Guido has grown used to Michele's temper and ignores his sharp comment. Guido eyes him seriously. 'Several times over the past few weeks, I have seen someone following us, or rather, following you.'

'And?'

'I believe this man is a professional, likely an assassin hired by the Roman family that no doubt seeks revenge against you. He is always alone and manages to blend with his surroundings, keeping himself hidden. He is clearly very skilled. I am lucky I saw him at all.'

'What do you suggest?'

'We must be more careful, more vigilant.'

'Guido, I have absolute trust in your ability to protect me, and my own ability to defend myself. I do possess skill with a rapier, you know.'

Guido nods. 'You show an uncanny skill at *painting* swords.' *A most backhanded compliment,* Michele figures. Guido continues in an attempt to soften the blow. 'In this case, I am sure both your skill as a swordsman and the quality of your steel, as well as my assistance, will be enough to ensure your safety. I simply thought that a further warning was called for.' Guido half-turns in his seat to signal the conversation is at an end.

———

'Ah, Signor Colonna, *buon giorno*. This is the first time you have come to my studio. Please have a seat.'

Michele hurries to clear several rags off a chair and takes a seat himself across from Duke Colonna. 'And, may I ask, what is the occasion for your visit?'

'I wanted to see how you are getting along. I apologize for taking so many weeks to come see you. I have been busy. You are comfortable here in the palazzo?' He glances at Guido and nods.

*Not weeks,* thinks Michele. *Several months.* 'Yes. Absolutely. My gratitude, like your generosity, is boundless.'

The duke sighs and looks at the painting Michele has been working on but makes no comment. 'A friend of mine has recently returned from Rome. I had asked him to make a few inquiries on your behalf.'

Michele leans forward from the edge of his seat. 'Was your friend able to meet with His Eminence Cardinal Del Monte? Did he mention if my remission will be issued soon?'

'Yes. The cardinal told him there has been little activity, unfortunately. I am sorry to bring bad news. I know it is not what you wish to hear, but there is something else. He heard that the Barefoot Carmelites, who commissioned a painting from you some time ago...'

'Yes, yes, *The Dead Virgin*.'

'He told me they have refused to hang the painting in church.'

Michele pulls back into his seat, shocked. 'Why? Does the cardinal know the cause?'

'No. He only knows that the refusal is being talked about in Rome. He has few details and could only report that your name was heard in rumours and gossip.'

'It becomes ever more important that I get back to Rome as soon as possible. I could perhaps make changes in the painting in order to please the Brothers.'

'I thought once an artist decided a painting was complete, there was no possible way to change it. Is it not true?'

'For some paintings, perhaps. But if the Brothers have good reason for refusing it, I would listen, of course. I would like to keep up a good relationship with the clergy.'

'And then run them through with your rapier? I have heard that your temper is legendary in Rome. I am a little surprised at your calm.'

'I have learned much in the past months, Your Excellency. I am a changed man. I try not to lock horns with those who are my patrons and offer to pay well for my art. I leave my scrapping for the streets.'

'I have heard nothing about any trouble since you have arrived in Naples. You seem to be avoiding run-ins with the locals.'

'Guido has turned out to be a good influence on me, a steady hand on my shoulder. I must thank you for his services.'

'It's nothing.' Duke Colonna waves at the air.

'Tell me, Your Excellency, I hear the Colonna family has a chapel here at the Church of San Lorenzo Maggiore, a chapel dedicated to the Madonna of the Rosary, yes?'

'It is true. Why do you ask?'

'To show my great gratitude, I would like to paint a Madonna of the Rosary for your chapel. Would it please you?'

'I suppose.'

Michele is surprised at the lack of enthusiasm in the duke's response. 'Then, I will start on it tomorrow. I will be sure to paint you a masterpiece.'

'*Grazie*,' Don Colonna mumbles while taking his leave.

———————

Three weeks later, Michele invites the duke to his studio to view the completed painting. Again, the duke nods, thanks him, and leaves, sending a servant later to fetch the work.

Michele puzzles over the duke's lack of response. *It is not my best painting perhaps, but surely, he could show a bit more gratitude.*

Late the next day, Michele walks with Guido along the seafront. The fresh wind whips up waves and blows salty drops into their faces. On this sunny day, there is a clear view of Vesuvius in the distance. Gulls tilt and swoop above, screeching at the two men who have invaded their private domain.

'Guido, let me ask you something. The painting I did for His Excellency—he seemed displeased with it. Do you know why?'

'I do not. But I do know this. The duke finds himself in financial difficulties these days. I hope I do not shock you to reveal that your painting is for sale.'

Michele stops short and stares at Guido. 'For sale?'

'Yes. Don Colonna is attempting to sell it. Due to your growing reputation, your work now fetches a good price on the open market. Do not be offended. The duke simply needs money.'

Michele turns, leans against the balustrade and gazes out at the choppy bay and its indigo waves edged with white lace, like the dresses of young Neapolitan girls on their way to church. He mumbles to himself. 'What am I doing here? I must get back to Rome.'

Guido hears Michele's words and says, 'You'd do well to forget about Rome for now, my friend. The duke says it is too soon to return. You would end up with your head on a pike.'

# ✦ THE ASSASSIN ✦

I have been following him now for months and even I, known for my endurance, begin to lose patience. But finally, a possible opening. The thought occurred to me while I was eating a bowl of tripe stew at a gloomy tavern in the early evening. After a couple pots of wine, I noticed that a beam of the setting sun had somehow avoided the surrounding buildings and entered the dark tavern. The shaft of light illuminated a table, deep in a corner of the murky room, at which sat two men. It reminded me of that painting the artist had been working on when I first modelled for him—the one in which I played Matthew, or rather Levi, the Jewish tax collector. The painter had made use of the available light, directing it as he pleased. While I finished my soup, the idea hit me. I have been keeping too much distance. I should show myself, announce myself, offer to be his model again here in Naples, and take my chances at finding my moment.

I have discovered that he has become friends with two other painters here in the city. Whenever they visit him in the afternoon, he does not appear on the street that evening or the next morning. In fact, a lamp is often left on all night in what I believe must be his studio in the palazzo. He must be inspired by his visits with these two other artists and want to paint after they leave. I will enter after they have gone and offer my services as a model. Various other people come to the palazzo who must be his models. I will gain entry by pretending to be one of them. I will tell him that I thought to offer myself as a model once again when I heard that he, too, was here in Naples.

Perhaps I should consider using poison. If I can get close and avoid his guard's eye, they would have no reason to suspect me. I could dump it in his ever-present glass of wine. But truly, what am I thinking? Poison? The tool of jealous wives and mad clergymen. No, a good, sharp blade will do for me. I have a small stiletto that fits into a secret slot in my boot. It is sharp enough to slit a man's throat.

———————

Gaining entry to the palazzo at the door is no problem. As far as the servant is concerned, I am just another model the artist has requested to come to his studio. The old, stooped footman leads me to the second level and down a hall. He opens a door wide and steps in. 'Sir, one of your models has arrived.'

'I am expecting no models today,' Merisi says as he stands before an easel, brush in hand. His guard is seated on a chair no more than four feet away, his keen eyes missing no detail of my face, my person.

I step around the servant and give a small bow. 'Master, it is I, Luca. I worked as a model for you in Rome, several times.'

'Luca? *Dio mio*. I could never forget that face. What are you doing here in Naples?'

'My brother who lives in the city has provided me some work,' I lie. 'But his business has come upon hard times. Word is that the great artist from Rome is now living and painting here in Naples. I thought perhaps you might be in need of an experienced model. As you may recall, I was skilled at holding my place for long periods.'

'I do remember. One of the best.' He pauses and turns back to study his painting. Meanwhile, the guard, Guido, is keeping a close eye on me. 'I should finish this work in a week or so and then I have plans for a crucifixion of Saint Andrew. I could use you as a model for the saint. That long, narrow face, that high forehead. I remember them well.'

I smile. 'I have posed as a saint before, as you know, and I also have experience at being crucified.'

Merisi snorts a short laugh. 'Ah, yes. The painting of Saint Peter. I ended up redoing that painting with a different model. You proved a

touch too young. But I think for Saint Andrew you will be perfect. What luck.'

He orders me to take off my shirt. 'I want to see your chest. You are thin. That is good. You have not been eating since your arrival in Naples?'

I give a grim smile.

'Hold your arms out as if you are about to be crucified.'

I do so.

He says, 'Perfect. I can see every one of your ribs. Keep to your diet for the next few weeks. I want you to maintain that emaciated look which appears so natural on you.'

I nod and put my shirt on, careful to hide my triumphant smile.

---

A little over a week later I am back in Merisi's studio. His guard stares at me, frowning.

The painter asks, 'You have been starving yourself, as I requested?'

'Yes. I feel like a stray dog roaming the streets looking for scraps of food to appease his hunger.' Merisi will never know how truly I speak, as I do feel like a cur much of the time. But my hunger is of a different sort, one that will not be satisfied with meat and drink. Only blood will nourish me, *his* blood. I imagine the feast I will throw for myself when I collect my final payment from the Tomassonis. Good wine, endless joints of meat, oranges, figs. My stomach rumbles as my imagination gorges itself.

'Good, good.' A wooden cross leans against the wall. It has been cut short so when I stand against it, my limbs are at the right height. 'Go to the cross and hold out your arms. I am ready to begin. First, take off your clothes and put on this loincloth.'

I remove my clothes and cinch the loincloth as directed. When I place my boots nearby, I take care that the small knife is not visible.

---

For days on end, Guido the guard never leaves the room. As long as I am there, he is there. The painter goes on with his work. I do my modelling, following Merisi's orders. I hold still and unmoving for hours. I am good at it, better than before in Rome. I am on the hunt, awaiting my moment. And finally, it comes.

At mid-afternoon, a servant appears at the door of the studio. He addresses the guard. 'The Master wishes that you come immediately to his chambers.'

Guido turns from the servant and looks at Merisi. 'But ...'

The servant takes a step into the studio. 'Master says you will not be gone for long, but he insists that he needs you now. Now.'

I realize that only a summons from the duke would cause Guido to abandon his station.

Guido says to the artist, 'I will return shortly.'

Merisi does not break his concentration, dipping his brush, staring at the canvas, then attacking it. The artist pauses and glances out the window. He seems to be looking out at the bay and turns his head to gaze at Vesuvius, visible in a corner of the window.

My chance has come at last. Once the echo of footsteps has faded down the hallway, I say, 'I have not moved in several hours. A moment to stretch? Would it be possible?'

Reluctantly, Merisi nods, and goes to his table covered with rags, paints, and brushes. His back is to me as he wipes a brush. I am barefoot for the modelling, so I slip on my boots, and smoothly slide the stiletto from its hiding place. Knife in hand, I lunge before the painter can turn. I grab his hair and pull back his head. He immediately struggles, which slows me slightly. I move to slit his throat, but before I can do so I am shoved hard in the back. I crash forward into the painter, who knocks into the table, toppling it.

Guido has returned sooner than expected! Leaping to my feet, I dash to the door. Guido, intent on ensuring that Merisi is unharmed, is trying to pull the artist out from beneath the overturned table. On my way to the door, I snatch up my clothes and hurry down the hall and into the street. I do not stop running for several dozen blocks. I dart down streets and alleys and across squares, not resting until I am assured that Guido does not follow. As I run, I notice that people look at me in shock—this maniac, this escapee from the madhouse fleeing in his loincloth and boots—and their astonishment and fear help to clear my way through the crowds. No one wishes to confront the fanatic. Their mouths agape, eyes wide, they step aside for me to hurtle past.

In an alley, I find a shadowy doorway where I can collapse. I'm panting like an old horse. It is then that I notice my foot. In my haste, I dropped the stiletto into my boot without securing it properly, and my foot is now badly cut. Removing my boot with difficulty, I pour out blood like wine from a flagon. I remove the loincloth and use it to bind the wound before throwing on my clothes. Watchful, I limp back to my hole.

The next morning when I awake, the entire foot is red and almost twice its normal size. I sweat although the room is cool. The walls, spinning...

# ❦ THE ARTIST ❦

---

Late in the afternoon, Michele is at work on a painting, a flagellation of Christ on order by the Church of San Lorenzo Maggiore. The attack by Luca is fading into the past. He has thrown himself into his work in the few weeks since the attack; it is the only thing that makes it possible for him to forget Luca's betrayal. He survived and that is all that matters. He has Guido's auspicious return to thank for that.

Michele steps toward the canvas, brush raised, a blue tear shining at the brush's tip. He pauses, deep in thought. *Why is it these Neapolitans seem to love pain and suffering and cruelty so much? They want nothing but crowns of thorns and whippings, crucifixions and death. All the passions of Christ and the martyrs. And here I am, in the shadow of Vesuvius, delivering it to them. What was it Mario said? It is the moment before the action that matters. That is where the power is most potent. I have been forced to ignore that dictum in Naples. Everything is finished in these works. Completed and done. I know well how to paint glowing skin, rapturous faces, tortured bodies, but nothing reveals that energy and power of awaiting the next moment, that sense of imminence, of being at the edge of destiny, like a warrior a moment before the battle begins, lovers a moment before climax, the bowman a moment before releasing the arrow. My earlier paintings revealed the lightning before the thunder, but these, these are thunder long after the lightning has passed. Still good in their way, I believe, but at their dismal end. A kind of fulfillment, yes, but followed inevitably by deterioration and decay.*

A servant comes to the door and announces His Excellency Duke Colonna. The duke enters.

'Welcome, Your Excellency. Please, make yourself comfortable.'

Michele recalls that the painting he created for the Colonna chapel has been sold. *Better not to mention it. I owe much to this man and he could easily put me out on the street.*

'I have several men out looking for this assassin. They will bring him to me soon, I am sure of it.'

'They will never find him,' he says without concern. 'In any case, Guido here,' he gestures at the guard, seated by the door, 'will no doubt continue to ensure my safety. I owe him my life.'

Guido nods slightly.

The duke glances at the painting. 'You seem to never cease working, Michele. Are you always so industrious?'

'I have a commission for this flagellation of Christ from the De Franchis for their chapel.' *And never any commission from the Colonna family. Why is that?* 'They seem to be in a rush to have it. Everyone is always in a hurry to get their works completed and installed. They must think I can turn out paintings of genius with the ease of a butcher slaughtering a pig.'

'Well then, let me get straight to the point. I have just returned from Rome.'

On hearing this, Michele turns away from his canvas and puts his brush down. 'Did you see Cardinal Del Monte? What news is there of my pardon?'

'In regards to your remission, His Eminence said that he himself and several other cardinals are working hard on it, but it is much too soon to return. I also heard that the Tomassonis have not given up their search for you. This Luca was likely sent by them. They know you are in Naples and they remain intent on exacting revenge. Exactly how they are going about that is a mystery, but it is widely known that you are working in my palazzo, under my protection.' He pauses. 'And something else has come to my attention.'

'Yes?'

'You know something of a painter named Rubens, from the Low Countries?'

'Yes, Peter Paul Rubens. I do know him. He is Flemish, in fact. I met him several times in Rome, where he now lives and works.'

'I never before heard his name. In any case, your painting that was refused by the Carmelites ...'

'*The Death of the Virgin*. What of it?'

'Rubens has announced to the world that it is a masterpiece. It has been sold to Duke Gonzaga of Mantua, but before delivery it was put on public display and has become a sensation in Rome. Del Monte asked me to mention it to you. Word of your considerable artistic abilities continues to spread. Your reputation is soaring.'

Though he says nothing, Michele thinks, *And it likely drove up the price you got for the* Madonna of the Rosary. Instead, he sighs. 'I really must get back to Rome.'

'You are not fond of Naples?'

Michele realizes he must be careful in his reply. He knows that diplomacy is not his strong suit. 'I am fond of Naples, of course, but Rome is where the art world has decided to gather. My supporters and patrons are there. You must understand that my life and work depend on my return to Rome.' He places his hand over his heart.

'Of course.' The duke smiles in a way that Michele finds insincere.

'Your Excellency, did His Eminence the Cardinal indicate how long I must wait for my pardon?'

'No. He mentioned that there have been some positive developments. And yet, there is still a price on your head. Perhaps not as great as the price on your paintings but still, a price.' The duke chuckles.

*Nothing humorous about this, you* cazzo. In another context, in another time of his life, Michele might have gone for his rapier in response to this little jest. Instead, he resists comment, snatches his brush from the table, and goes back to work.

———

Several weeks later, a servant enters Michele's studio in the morning and announces: 'This afternoon, His Excellency requests that the master come to his study. He would like you to meet with a relative of his.'

'Who?'

'Regrettably, master, I cannot answer your question.'

Later that day, Michele shuffles out of his spattered painting tunic and dresses in his finest clothes. He sensed earlier by the servant's tone that this would be an important meeting. He wonders if it might be another commission. He leaves his studio at the appointed time, hurries to the duke's spacious chambers and is announced by a servant. As he enters, he sees a well-dressed man, about his own age, waiting on a settee.

'Michelangelo Merisi, I would like to introduce you to my cousin, Fabrizio Sforza Colonna.' Michele nods his head and notes that the man has a weathered face and sharp black eyes. He gives the artist an intelligent, appraising look as Michele takes the seat offered him by the duke.

Portraits of the ancient Colonna family line the walls of the study. Michele feels claustrophobic and uncomfortable; the dour images stare down at him in judgment. He believes he has been purposely given a seat in the room where all eyes are on him, as if he is guilty of some dire malfeasance and the Colonnas are a huge panel of judges expressing their disappointment in him, this errant member of the Merisi family.

'It has come to my attention,' the duke begins, 'that a certain man in Naples is asking about you. Not the artist's model who attacked you, but another. It seems that the Tomassoni family has hired a second assassin to try to exact revenge. I hear that they tire of waiting so long for this Luca to accomplish his vile deed. Also, as I mentioned, it has become common knowledge in Rome that you are now staying in Naples under my protection.' Michele realizes the duke is reiterating this information for the benefit of his cousin. He continues. 'We would like to suggest a more secure refuge.'

Michele feels a quiver of anxiety, wondering where they will send him. 'And where would that be, Your Excellency?'

Fabrizio Colonna speaks for the first time. 'The island of Malta.'

'Malta?' Michele is unable to keep the alarm out of his voice. 'Why Malta? That's even further from Rome than Naples. The only fact I claim to know about Malta is the story of the great siege when the Maltese defeated the Turks.'

Fabrizio speaks, his voice calm and even: 'I am not surprised at your ignorance of the place as it is somewhat out of the way. But Malta proves convenient because my galley is sailing there tomorrow morning. You would have protected passage.'

'Again, I ask, why Malta?'

The duke interjects. 'Malta is ruled by the Sovereign Military Hospitaller Order of St John, commonly known as the Knights of Saint John. The knights come from Spain, France, Italy, Germany and the Low Countries. Many of the foreigners understand and speak our tongue. Fabrizio is the admiral for the order. The island is extremely secure. The Grand Master of the order, the French nobleman, Alof de Wignacourt, has heard of your fame and has requested your services as an artist.'

Fabrizio leans forward from his seat. 'Several commissions await you, one a portrait of the Grand Master himself. This is a great honour.'

Michele decides that he likes this Fabrizio. Unlike the duke, he talks only to convey information, adds nothing extra.

The duke continues, 'Something else has arisen. A distant possibility.' He glances at his cousin. 'I hear that you could be offered a knighthood in the order. Also, you should know that the Knights have good contacts in Rome and would be of tremendous assistance in your obtaining a pardon.'

Michele decides on the spot. 'I will go to Malta as you suggest. But Your Excellency, I have one request and one only—I wish to bring Guido along with me.'

The duke leans back in his chair, pondering this development. 'I have given my word to His Eminence, Cardinal Del Monte, that I will protect you. As you wish, Guido may go with you. But please know that this is not a permanent arrangement.'

'I understand,' Michele replies. 'I do not plan to be there for long. I am sure my pardon will come soon.'

———————

The next morning, early, under cloudy skies threatening rain, Fabrizio Colonna arrives in a carriage to collect Michele and his baggage. He leaps down from a seat beside the driver to greet Michele and Guido. While Guido loads several bags and a trunk, Michele and Fabrizio discuss the length of the journey. All three men then step up into the carriage. As Fabrizio enters and sits, he sticks his head out the door and instructs the driver, 'Proceed to the harbour, to my galley.'

They soon arrive at the harbour, a forest of masts not far down the curve of the bay. Several fishing boats, sails nearly slack, struggle out to sea in the faint breeze. Michele climbs out of the carriage while Fabrizio strides toward his galley to prepare for departure. Guido insists on dealing with the baggage himself. In the grey light, Michele sees around the bay the stout medieval fortress, Castello Angiono, with its five round sandstone turrets. In the distance beyond, across the sea, Vesuvius belches a banner of smoke that disappears into the sky.

In the other direction, beyond the harbour, he notices four fishermen standing in a line on the beach hauling on a rope. For some reason he himself does not understand, Michele watches as they strain to pull in a heavy, knotted net, cords of muscle in their hands and necks bulging. As they pull it in, the net is speckled with a few flopping fish. One of the fish catches Michele's eye. Even at this distance, he can hear it on the beach barking like a dog, twisting and gasping as it expires, drowning on air.

# ⊰ THE ASSASSIN ⊱

---

'Who enters my room? Who are you?' I am sprawled on my mat, soaked in sweat. I can barely open my eyes, which are crusted over. I have no idea how long I have been here.

'Do not be alarmed.'

I discover it is the matron, my landlady, who comes each month to collect the coins for this miserable hole I inhabit. My head is pounding. I try to bark at her but my voice comes out strangled. 'You come ... for the rental ... payment? Come back later ... when I am well.'

She shakes her head. 'You misunderstand. You have not been out of this room for weeks. Your limbs are like sticks. All day and night you rave in a fever, keeping my other tenants awake. I have brought the local priest again to help you. At first, we thought you had contracted *mal aria*, the evil air, as you seemed to have cold fever in the morning and hot fevers in the eve, but then we noticed your foot.'

Behind her a bent, elderly priest stands, waiting and holding something in his hands. I manage to shout at him. 'Do you dare bring ... the oil for the last rites? Get out! Get out!'

The priest inches forward. 'Quiet, my son. Be at peace. I do not carry the extreme unction but a bowl of broth for you. This kind lady has been treating the terrible wound in your foot. She replaced the rushes on the floor with fresh ones and scattered some mulberry twigs to attract the fleas away from your bedding. Over the past few weeks, we have been feeding you thin soup and giving you water, but you barely opened your eyes. When you did finally open them, they seemed to be viewing horrors that I cannot imagine. I thought you were perhaps possessed by a demon. I almost called in an exorcist, but then you settled. Here.' He struggles down onto one knee to offer me a spoonful of broth. I stare at him, his soft, grey eyes; then I slurp from the spoon. I swallow with difficulty. 'How long have I been here?'

'Several weeks, as I said,' the matron responds.

'Drink.' The priest comes with another spoonful and I swallow it. I am too tired to ask any more questions, and before I finish half the broth, my heavy head has fallen back onto the mat.

My back arches and my breath convulses as if I am trying to swallow the entire sky. I recover and stare at the ceiling. 'I must get dressed and go out. I have work to accomplish. *Someone I must find ...*' That last part, I am unsure if I say it aloud or think it.

'No, my son,' the priest warns. 'You need rest in order to recover your strength. It will be a while yet before you are well.'

'Padre ...' I attempt speech once again. 'I saw ... I saw an hourglass. The grains of sand seemed to fall more and more slowly and when they fell, they crashed down with the sound of a mountain avalanche. Then I heard men's laughter, and it sounded like the chaotic clanging of bells in hell. Am I dying?'

'No. I do not believe so. I fear you came close enough to hear God whispering your name, but you retreated from that abyss.'

'The Devil.'

'What's that?' the cleric asks.

'It was not God whispering my name. I am sure it was Satan.'

---

After weeks of daily visits from the priest, and occasional visits from the motherly matron to check on my foot, I begin to feel healthy again. One morning, I am able to sit up. The next day I can stand and dress myself. The day after that, I return to the streets near Duke Colonna's palazzo and renew my hunt for the artist, but I can stand only an hour before a fatigue washes over me and I must return to my mat. In that hour, I saw nothing. No one entering or leaving the palazzo, no movement inside.

The next day, I am able to wait three hours but still, I notice nothing. On the third day, I watch from late afternoon until midnight and still nothing. No sign of Merisi or his guard, and no light from his studio window. Again, the fourth day, nothing. As if he has disappeared from the world. I decide to consult Aldo, my Neapolitan 'ear' and source of information.

I enter the tavern where, in his quiet way, he holds court. I toss a few coins onto the table. Just like his compatriot in Rome, he taps the table for more. 'Anyone working for the Tomassonis must have the wherewithal to pay more than these few coins.'

I'm surprised that he knows who has hired me, but I say nothing and add a couple more coins to the pile. 'Where is the artist Michelangelo Merisi, the one who was hiding at the palazzo of Duke Colonna?'

'Ah, the artist from Rome. I will ask around. Return to me tomorrow and I am sure I will have the information you seek.'

The next day I return in late afternoon.

My source of information is at his usual table. I walk in and take a seat close by.

He glances up. 'My sources tell me the artist has gone. He has left Naples.'

'Gone? Where? Back to Rome?'

'No. I am told he has gone to the isle of Malta. You have heard of this place? He is now under the protection of the Knights Hospitaller. And his guard, the duke's man, has gone with him.'

'Malta? *Dio mio.*'

'Another bit of information about the Tomassonis that will be of tremendous interest to you, I am sure.' Again, he taps the table three times with his finger and again I place a few more coins before him. 'The Tomassonis believe you have failed in your quest to find the artist. They have hired another to accomplish the task.'

'What?!' This comes as a complete surprise to me. I realize I have been invisible, that is, ill and recovering for five or six weeks. Another assassin … that is disturbing news. The man across the table from me finishes his wine and calls for another jug. *Malta? I know nothing of the place and am not confident I will find an 'ear' there to give me the information I need. I ask myself, should I follow or wait in Naples for his return?*

The man adds, 'The artist has his hopes set on a pardon from Rome, you know.'

'I suspected, yes.'

'As soon as it comes through, it is said he will return.'

I picture my final payment from the Tomassonis disappearing into the air.

## ⊰ THE ARTIST ⊱

After an uneventful journey, Fabrizio Colonna's galley arrives at Malta, an island of sandstone about fifty miles from Sicily and not far from the coast of North Africa. Forbidding, high stone walls greet them at the harbour of Valletta, the capital city. Michele finds nothing inviting about the place, with its houses of tan-coloured stone, its steep streets, and its painful light. He senses some distinct foreign influence, a darkness both intriguing and disturbing, behind the sharp, brilliant sun.

Following an effusive and complimentary introduction from Fabrizio Sforza Colonna, the Grand Master of the Knights, Alof de Wignacourt offers Michele and Guido a studio and accommodations within his own fort in Valletta. Wignacourt is clearly pleased to have a painter of such fame in his service. Michele finds that he is being passed along from one powerful patron to another, and that his star continues to rise. After taking a few days to settle in and establish his studio, Michele begins work on a portrait of the Grand Master.

An immediate connection forms between Michele and this

vigorous Frenchman of sixty years. His manner displays both power and confidence, and these prove attractive to Michele. The Grand Master is aware of Michele's crime in Rome and does not seem to be bothered by it. Michele guesses that this attitude is due to Wignacourt's own experience—he himself has probably cut off a few heads in battle. And perhaps the painter's crime serves to prove to the soldier that Michele is not an artist of weak temperament but a man who does whatever must be done.

Over the next several months, Michele enjoys the camaraderie of the knights who seem to take to him. And Wignacourt is thrilled with the portrait.

Wignacourt finds another painting for Michele to undertake, as well as a small church commission. Then one day, without Michele suggesting it, the Grand Master surprises Michele by offering to write to his own ambassador in Rome about the status of the artist's pardon. Michele is hopeful that an intervention from this powerful man will expedite his return to Rome.

———

A dour-faced servant comes into the Grand Master's formal, private meeting chambers and, from a crystal decanter, pours thick red wine into a pair of heavy Venetian glasses. *Wine the colour of blood,* Michele muses. Michele feels settled in Valletta and accepted by the Order, and yet, no matter how agreeable his life on Malta, Michele never forgets he has been banished from his life in Rome.

Across the table from him, Wignacourt sits, the star of the Order on his tunic, a confident half-smile on his face. 'We have something to celebrate today,' he announces.

Michele edges up straighter in his seat. 'Yes? What is it we are celebrating, my Lord?'

'I have decided that now is the time to confer upon you a knighthood in the Order of Saint John.'

Michele, a surprised yet pleased look on his face, says. 'But I have only been resident here for a short while. As I understand it, all four of one's grandparents must be noble to allow entry. And I was under the impression that all candidates must first serve time on the galleys, fighting the Turks. Am I expected to take ship and serve?'

'Would you be willing to do so?'

Michele fingers the stem of the glass. 'Of course,' he lies. He wonders if Wignacourt noticed his slight hesitation. *I rather enjoy fighting occasionally in the streets, but would hate to battle the Turks for months on end. It would further delay my return to Rome.*

'That is good to hear but it will not be necessary. I have been watching you closely since your arrival. I am impressed. I have decided that none of the usual requirements will be needed in your case. You are a man of uncommon—what shall I call it—valour? Yes, valour and dignity, and immense talent. As I understand it, many of the other knights are fond of you and, rather than spending your time repelling the Saracen menace from the east, I would prefer that you stay right here and paint. I believe you are now one of the best-known artists in all of the Christian lands and you bring great esteem to the Order and our island.'

'I am honoured and gratified, My Lord.'

'Let us drink to it.'

They raise their glasses, toast, and drink.

Wignacourt places two thick fingers on the base of his heavy, long-stemmed glass. 'The ceremony will take place in two weeks. In the meantime, I would like you to do something for me, and for the Order.'

'Anything, my lord.' Michele is elated—a knighthood, what could be better? Yet, he feels trapped by the Grand Master's beneficence, trapped on this island. He is being granted an immense gift, without having to earn it in the customary way. At the same time, he is losing a modicum of his freedom, like a fish netted in the sea and dumped in a small garden pool.

Wignacourt continues: 'I would like you to paint our Order's patron, Saint John the Baptist for the Conventual Church of Saint John here in Valletta.'

'I would be greatly honoured. A painting of Saint John, then. I will begin on the morrow. But what of the crime of which I am accused in Rome? Does that not perhaps make a knighthood difficult, if not impossible?'

'That is of no importance for an artist such as yourself. I am told that a pardon, from the Pope himself, will not be long in coming.' The Grand Master thinks for a moment. 'One other thing—I need a new standard for my ship, and I want you to paint it.'

## ⊰ THE ASSASSIN ⊱

My plan to stay in Naples to await Merisi's return has changed. My funds are dwindling. I need my final payment from the Tomassonis. And now this word of a second assassin pressures me to complete my task. I go again to see Aldo, my 'ear' in Naples, to find out what he knows about Malta.

From Aldo I learn more than I ever needed to know about the island, the Maltese and the Knights who rule them. Aldo is a strange man who loves to talk; he is infatuated with the sound of his own voice. How he obtains his vast store of knowledge, I have no idea.

He says he has a contact in Malta who will help me—for a price, of course. Everything has a price, and my money runs through my fingers like thin wine. I have just enough coin to make a journey to Malta possible. 'But,' he explains, 'I must point out that the Knights Hospitaller keep a close eye on those coming and going from their island. And getting into their forts and castles is impossible. The Grand Master's fort is impregnable. However, you have one advantage: the contact I am giving you is a native Maltese. The Maltese hate the Knights for taking over their island.'

The next day I board a ship for Malta.

---

I have no trouble avoiding interrogation on entry to Valletta. There are times when I believe I can make myself invisible, or, if not invisible, then so commonplace and ordinary as to be beneath anyone's notice. I explain that I have come to visit my elderly mother and the eyes of the guards glaze over. I am into the city with ease.

That night, I make contact with Aldo's associate.

He has a swarthy look, not unlike Sicilians I have known, but with a bit of Moorish or Arabic blood thrown in. My eye is drawn to his small, fidgety hands. His information comes cheap, compared to Aldo's in Naples, and certainly compared to Carlo's in Rome.

He repeats everything my Neapolitan informant has told me. 'The fort? Yes, impregnable.'

'Have you seen or heard anything about this artist from Rome?'

'Yes, but not much. I possess no information on where he stays, but if you are willing to wait, I will make inquiries tomorrow.'

Later, I find a hole in the wall in which to lay my head, following a meal of putrid-smelling squid and raw wine.

The next afternoon, my head pounding, I find my contact on the steps of the Church of Saint John. Valletta is a city of stone. Every street, every wall, every building, the same smooth, tan-coloured stone.

'Your painter, he is living in the fort of the Grand Master.'

'The fort which I keep hearing is impregnable?'

'Yes. He has lived there since he arrived on Malta, I believe. He is seen often in the taverns of the town and has had run-ins several times with some of the knights. Nothing serious. A bit of swordplay, that is all. He was recently made a knight in the Order. I also know that the artist is working on a large painting for this very church.'

'Anything else?'

'Only that he is generally liked among the knights, although …'

'What is it?'

'There are some among the knights who believe he is unworthy of his knighthood. It was granted to him without any of the usual requirements. No service on the galleys against the Turks. Most importantly, he has no noble blood. They say it is thinning the purity of the Order, even if he is a famous artist. They say he has only become a knight because the Grand Master is fond of him and desires the world to know that the Order can command the work of great artists. They believe that a knighthood should be based on bravery and courage, not artistic talent.'

'Is the Grand Master aware of this resentment among his men?'

'Yes, he must be aware of it. At the ceremony installing Merisi as a knight, I heard there was one young fellow, a well-known troublemaker, who shouted out, "He's a murderer wanted in Rome! Not a knight at all. He is not deserving." The young knight was dragged from the room by the guards and put in jail for several days. He still goes about the town attacking the reputation of the artist.'

'I see. Is the painter's guard with him?'

'The giant?'

'Yes, the giant.'

'He is with the painter at all times, yes. The one never goes anywhere without the other.'

My heart sinks at this news and I let out a deep sigh. 'Your information is good? Trustworthy?'

'Have no doubt.'

I give the man a few coins. I tell him where I am staying and to let me know immediately if he learns anything more about the artist in the Grand Master's fort.

# ⊰ THE ARTIST ⊱

---

One evening, Michele and Guido are drinking together in a tavern where a number of knights are gathered at various tables around the room. The knights stamp their feet and pound their fists as they boast about fighting the Saracens on the island of Rhodes. Michele and Guido sit alone and talk quietly, Michele glancing occasionally at a frieze of French and Spanish knights in conversation, standing along the wall.

Suddenly, a young, drunken knight stumbles across the room and approaches their table. Guido holds his hand out, both to support the drunk and to keep him at bay. Michele recognizes him as a young French knight from a famous noble family, the one who made an unpleasant scene at his investiture.

'Look who drinks here among us.' He speaks loud enough for the entire room to hear as he gestures at Michele. The conversations among the knights trail off into silence at this interruption. 'Look at the bastard. The one who has gained a knighthood for no good reason. He did nothing to earn it. He simply made friends with the Grand Master. And, he's a murderer!'

'Silence yourself, friend,' says Guido, 'before you land yourself in trouble you cannot handle.'

Michele, his hand on the hilt of his rapier, stares intently at the Frenchman. He speaks in a low voice to the blond-haired knight, nodding at Guido, 'Listen to my friend. He tells the truth.'

The drunken knight ignores the warning. 'That painting of yours that hangs in our church—a scandal, a sacrilege, an insult to our Order and our religion. You are a fake, a blasphemous fake. You are not even a competent artist.'

Had the knight returned to his friends, it could have ended there. But it does not end there.

Leaning into Michele's face, the knight shouts, 'You boast no noble blood, no noble ancestors! And what you are doing to the Grand Master's page … unspeakable!' He straightens up and announces loudly to the crowd. 'He has been sodomizing the boy! This, this, commoner, is sodomizing a child of French nobility!' He leans down again and spits in Michele's face.

Guido barks so the crowd can hear, 'He lies! No one has touched the page.' But Michele draws his sword with a ringing sound, and in one swift motion, slashes the knight's left arm. The lower part of the arm and the left hand fall to the floor. He could kill the young knight, drunk as he is, on the spot, but Michele holds back. The Frenchman falls in a heap, grasping his arm, blood gushing between his fingers. The room erupts, and Michele instantly finds himself under the weight of five burly knights pinning him to the floor. Guido tries to throw them off, but there are too many for him to manage alone. Failing to release his friend, he flees, casting two knights aside as he runs out the door. With unerring instinct, Guido knows that he will be more help to Michele if he is not arrested with his friend and maintains his freedom.

A short while later, three knights drag Michele into Fort Sant'Angelo and stand him up before Wignacourt. The Grand Master's face is crimson as he shouts at the artist: 'I befriended you and supported you from the moment you arrived on Malta, and this is the way you repay me? Damn your eyes, damn you to hell!' The knights then force Michele down a ladder and into the *guva*, a bell-shaped, deep prison hole dug out of the rock underneath the fort. They remove the ladder and leave Michele in near-darkness.

Meanwhile, Guido rushes to the chambers of Fabrizio Sforza Colonna and explains what has happened. Colonna is a close friend of the director of the Order's prisons. 'I know that young knight Michele injured,' Fabrizio says to Guido. 'He's a troublemaker, an arrogant hothead hated by the older knights. I was warned that the artist had an uncontrollable temper, but I have sworn to the duke and the cardinal to protect him. Let us see what we can do.'

Two days later, Michele sits depressed in the dark when he notices a rope lowered into the *guva*. He hears Guido's voice from above. 'Master, I have bribed the guards. Climb out quickly.' Soon, Michele and Guido are scaling down a high stone wall outside the fort. At the bottom of the wall, a boat awaits them, rocking on the water. Four sailors row them to Colonna's galley, as they watch the sails of the larger boat being unfurled. Soon they are skimming over open water, under a curve of moon gleaming like a Turk's scimitar, heading for Sicily.

## ⁌ THE ASSASSIN ⁍

'He is gone, the painter. He has fled Malta.' My informant stands in the open doorway of my room, the stark sunlight of early morning shining behind him. I watch from my rough, straw-covered pallet, having just startled from sleep.

Leaning up on an elbow, I shake my head awake. 'What!? What do you mean? Where has he gone?'

'He was in a scuffle with one of the knights several evenings past. He was jailed in the *guva*.'

'Several nights ago!? And you didn't inform me?'

My informant shrugs his shoulders. 'I was away, fishing.'

'Fool.' I swing my feet to the floor and sit on the side of the pallet. Calmer now, I ask him, 'The *guva*? What is that?'

The Maltese explains. 'The *guva* is a prison hole dug out of stone beneath the fort. They lower a ladder for the prisoner to climb down and then remove it. The pit is inescapable.'

'Everything on this damnable island is either impregnable or inescapable. How did he escape then?'

'He must have had help.'

'From whom?'

The Maltese shrugs again and shakes his head.

'Does anyone know where he has gone?'

'He is clearly no longer on Malta. The Grand Master has sent his knights off in every direction to search for him. But no one knows where he has gone.'

'How can no one know?'

My head is spinning, trying to keep track of my prey. *I will return to Naples and wait. What else can I do?*

'Leave me.' I motion for him to go away.

I resolve to flee Malta as soon as possible.

## ⊰ THE ARTIST ⊱

'You have done well, Mario.' Michele and his friend and former apprentice, Mario, are finishing up a meal of white fish and cooked greens in the courtyard of Mario's simple house in Siracusa. A flagon of wine sits on the table between them. Mario refills Michele's cup. Mario's young Sicilian wife is busy inside. Guido squats on a stool by the door, alert as ever.

'A comfortable house and garden, a proud wife, success as a painter. I am impressed, Mario. And this is a lovely town. When we were passing by the harbour, I was surprised to see so many handsome fishing boats.'

'Yes. I can thank my father-in-law for my success here. He is well-off and well-connected. I owe my many commissions to him.'

A few clouds dot the whitish-blue sky above the garden wall

and the salt tang of the sea is on the air. Mario continues. 'You miss Fillide, yes?'

'Of course. I have a tremendous longing to get back to her, and to Rome. It has been over two years since I left. Before I was forced to flee, we were discussing possibly marrying. I try not to think of all the men who seek her affections, but sometimes it comes on me suddenly and I nearly weep for sorrow.'

'The painting of Saint John the Baptist that you mentioned you did on Malta, you were happy with it?'

'Yes, very much so. The painting was not at all what the Grand Master anticipated. Though, once he had recovered from his shock, he was quite happy with the result. I didn't know it at first but the painting turned out to be the payment that Wignacourt expected for my appointment as a Knight of Obedience in the Order of Saint John. I was invested several months ago. They love ceremony and ritual, these knights. They were all there, from the many realms of Christendom, to witness my investiture. I was deeply impressed and honoured. At the same time, it bothered me that he expected me to deliver this painting, as if I owed it to him. And, can you believe it, he wanted me to paint him a standard for his ship. A standard! I wanted to shout at him: I am no artisan! I am an artist! I do not paint banners and flags.' Michele paused. 'A Knight of Obedience. Mario, have you ever known me to be one for whom obedience is imperative? I am always driven to deliver the unexpected, to shock and surprise.'

'What did you depict in the painting of John, then?'

'The beheading of John the Baptist. His moment of martyrdom. The executioner grasps the knife in his hand, beside him a woman holds a wide bowl ready for the head. Nearby, an older woman stands with her hands at the sides of her head as if in horror, and another man, a soldier, watches. And from the side, a prisoner peers at them from a barred window. It is the largest painting I have ever done. I chose one of the cramped stone courtyards on Malta to stage the drama.'

'You say the Grand Master was pleased with it?'

'He was. He gave me a gift of a gold chain, and two slaves that I sold the next day on the market. I cannot have slaves trailing along behind me or watching me paint. I would find it a burden.' Michele pauses to empty his cup of wine and refill Mario's cup and his own from the flagon on the table. 'But something exceedingly strange happened when I finished that painting. I had a powerful feeling that it was me under the blade about to lose my head, and that it was me also wielding the knife.'

'Yes, that is odd.' Thoughtfully, Mario drinks. He gives Michele a studied look. 'I sense that you have something else to tell me, having arrived here without any message to announce your coming.'

'I do, in fact. Just two days ago I escaped the prison on Malta, after I was forced to give a young knight a taste of my sword. I slashed his arm clean off. It was foolish. I lost my head, but the knight was baiting me. I acted on impulse.'

'Do they know that you have come to Sicily?'

'No. I have numerous friends in the Order, and the knight I injured is widely disliked. The admiral of the Order himself, of the Colonna family, arranged for my escape on one of his ships and brought me here. He does not speak well of Wignacourt, the Grand Master. I suspect he has plans to become head of the Knights himself.'

'Would they not know that their galley left when you did?'

'The timing was sheer luck. The galley was scheduled to sail to Sicily at dawn. I suppose the ship was gone before anyone noticed I was missing from the prison. The guards who took the bribes had fled, so there was no one to raise the alarm. They would have no reason to believe I was aboard Colonna's ship.'

Mario relaxes and flashes a wry smile. 'You will never change, will you?'

'No.' Michele smiles to himself as he watches a tattered black crow settle on the wall beyond the garden of simples and herbs. The bird is staring at him from its left eye, its look oddly penetrating. *A sign?* he wonders, *or perhaps Wignacourt possesses the ability to train birds as spies.* He shakes the mad thought from his head, but his mood has darkened.

'I will be honest with you, Mario. I must be extremely careful. I am a hunted man. I sleep with one eye open and dagger in hand. In Naples, an assassin was searching for me because of the mistake I made in Rome, and now I am sure the knights, too, will be seeking this poor artist's head. As we sailed, I had a long talk with Colonna on the galley. He wondered that it was a bit too easy to arrange my escape, that perhaps Wignacourt preferred me to leave Malta rather than have his little noble page face the embarrassment of being dragged through the mud. The boy's family would not have appreciated that. Colonna added that I should maintain extreme caution, that Wignacourt perhaps allowed me to escape so that he could have me killed elsewhere, with the least dishonour to the Order. Honour, you see, is extremely important to them. In any case, I must return to Rome as soon as possible. I will resume and solidify my artistic career, and reunite with Fillide. But I fear I must return to Naples first, though the knights will certainly look for me there. All of which leads me to ask, while I delay my return to Naples, can you find any work for me here? A small commission perhaps?'

---

Mario is scheduled to do a painting for Giovanni Battista de' Lazzari, a wealthy trader originally from Genoa, who now lives in Messina. However, the younger painter has other work he prefers to do closer to home. Mario sends a message to Messina suggesting that his friend, Michelangelo Merisi da Caravaggio, take over the commission. The trader has heard of the famous painter from Rome and replies that he would be proud to have his chapel in the Messina church display a painting by such an artist.

Accompanied by Guido, Michele and Mario travel to Messina to further discuss the painting. On arriving at the trader's house, they are ushered into a spacious sitting room where the walls are covered with oil paintings in expensive frames, including a painting by Mario of the Virgin and Child.

Dressed in a gold-threaded waistcoat and smooth leather slippers, the jowly Lazzari welcomes the two men and asks them to be seated on a divan backed with cushions of purple silk. The servant pours wine into three silver cups. Lazzari says, 'I desire a painting of Saint John the Baptist for the chapel, to represent my given name.'

Michele glances at Mario, then turns his gaze to the trader. 'I would like to honour your wishes, Signore, but, unfortunately, I have just recently completed a large painting of the Baptist and would much prefer to work on a new subject if at all possible.'

'I see.'

The trader looks like a man who is used to getting his way. Michele adds, 'May I propose another subject? Why not make use of your patronymic instead of your given name? Lazzari is suggestive of Lazarus, who was an astonishing character from the Bible. I would love to paint a scene of the raising of Lazarus from the dead. It would demonstrate to all the strength and divine favour of your house.'

Lazzari hesitates. 'I was hoping for a John the Baptist.'

Michele feels uneasy; he needs the money the commission will bring. After a moment's silence, Lazzari nods his head. 'I have decided. I will have Mario do John the Baptist and you can paint me a Lazarus.'

Later, as Mario and Michele bump along in the carriage on their return to Siracusa, Guido sitting across from them, the younger painter breaks the silence, 'Why a painting of Lazarus? What about that subject appeals to you?'

Michele stares out the window a moment at the sere countryside. A few dusty trees in the distance, a scattering of sheep standing in their thin, spiky shade. 'I was in that hole on Malta for two days and two nights, my friend. There was almost no light at all, except for a faint glow when they brought me my gruel. I thought I was a dead man. Following my escape, as I stood on the galley and the first wind caught the sails sending us out to open sea, dawn was just breaking. That dawn light was my salvation. I realized I was, myself, Lazarus. I had been raised from the dead.' Michele pauses. 'Now, can you get me a fresh corpse to use as a model?'

———————

While in Sicily, Michele gains several more commissions—two Nativities painted in his rough, dark, earthy style. The payment for the Nativities is generous. He never ceases painting, fills his days with obsessive labour, working himself to exhaustion.

Wignacourt's knights are much on his mind during the months on Sicily. In fact, he is starting to mistrust everyone around him, and his temper, even more than usual, flares at the slightest provocation. A meek priest comes to negotiate a small commission for his rural church. Michele shouts at him for interrupting his work. The priest flees, skirts flapping like a flock of crows startled from a bush.

During a long stormy night of flashing nightmares, Michele again and again bolts upright in bed, convinced he hears disturbing sounds. His grip on his stiletto is white-hot. He is sure an assailant has entered his room. Time and again, it proves to be nothing: a nightjar on the roof, a mouse in the wall, Guido snorting in his sleep. Michele's heart hammers like heavy rain on the sea.

———————

The world seems to speed quickly downhill. The days rush by, and every night feels like an endless, interminable horror. After saying a quick farewell to Mario, Michele and Guido board a ship and head back to Naples under a grey and brooding sky. A low patch of cloud exhibits the rolled and twisted look of entrails. *It has been long enough. It is time to start the journey back to Rome. Only in Rome can things*

*come right, only in Rome will I have my old life back. Only in Rome will I be protected and safe. But first, I must stop in Naples. From there I will contact the Cardinal and learn if my return to Rome is possible. It has been so long, they must be awaiting me. My pardon likely came through while I was gone, or so I hope.*

Guido stands across the narrow deck behind him as Michele gazes straight down at the water. First, he glimpses his reflection in the water, but then he sees the sea forming a whirlpool, swirling down and down, spiralling to the bottom, until all the sea's water disappears, sluicing and slipping into a hole. The boat on which he stands remains unaffected. He cannot surmise what this vision might mean, if it is a sign of some sort. Strange images such as this have been coming to him lately. He wipes sweat from his brow.

Once they arrive in Naples, Michele and Guido return to the palazzo of Duke Colonna, who welcomes the painter without hesitation. The duke says, 'Once you left Malta, no one knew where you were. I have received several letters from Cardinal Del Monte seeking information about you. I was embarrassed to think that my good friend might believe I had lost track of you. He says he has news. But I heard there was trouble on Malta and that you fled. Where did you go?'

'Sicily, Your Excellency.' Michele provides no explanation. His heart has leapt at word of a communication from Del Monte. 'But, tell me the news from His Eminence. It must be my pardon.'

'His letters merely requested that you write to him as soon as possible. I suggest you send him a letter and let him know you are again in my house in Naples. I am sure he will respond speedily.'

## ❧ THE ASSASSIN ❧

---

He has returned to Naples, as I knew he would. Once again, he lives in the palazzo of Duke Colonna, and I take up my post as if the past year never happened.

I am back in the hovel where the kindly matron and the priest helped me to recover. I am just able to pay for my room. A few small robberies have proved helpful—several gold implements I stole from a poorly guarded church were especially lucrative. The landlady is generous with her leftover food, bringing me a plate in the evening. I guess since she saved me once she now feels responsible for my well-being. I marvel that some people have goodness in their hearts but I do not question it. Her kindness might be as catching as the plague.

I notice that Merisi has returned to his painting. His persistence astounds me and is matched only by my own. I see his light on in the studio at all hours. It seems he never sleeps. I suspect I have to make my move soon or I will fail. Still, I am as patient as the sea. But, after my attack in his studio, I must take special care not to be seen.

---

Three days after the artist's return to Naples, I see the artist and Guido leave the palazzo at dusk. The sky is a dusty orange along the horizon to the west, as if a reflection of the flames of hell has been unveiled. I follow at a professional distance, feeling the fistful of fine sand which fills the left pocket of my waistcoat, the only pocket without holes. My plan is to fling the sand into Guido's eyes, blinding him long enough for me to dispatch Merisi. It might seem a desperate move if I had not used it once before with excellent results in Perugia. I was able to slice one brother while the other tore at his blinded eyes.

After a while, Merisi and Guido turn onto a long, narrow street that heads downhill toward the harbour. There is only one place they could be headed on this street: the most popular tavern in all of Naples, the Cerriglio. With the amount of time I have spent in Naples, I have learned the city's maze of streets by heart, so I take another route to get ahead of them as they saunter down the slope and before they reach the tavern. Soon I stand waiting in an alley a distance ahead—I can see the two of them walking towards me—and I ready myself for the ambush.

What happens next is completely unexpected. I see a man leap from a narrow balcony above the street and land on Guido's back, knocking him to one knee. The attacker tries to plant a stiletto in the guard's neck, but in the fall, he has missed and stuck it into Guido's left arm instead. Guido's next move is instantaneous and deadly. He swings his right arm and elbow high behind him with astonishing speed and power, breaking the man's neck. I can hear the crack from a distance. I watch the man go limp. Meanwhile four assailants with swords drawn have attacked Merisi. While Guido is engaged, the painter is at their mercy. While the artist defends himself ably against one of them, another slashes him in the face, once, twice, across the cheek, across the forehead. Another thrusts a sword into his right leg, another his left arm. Merisi is on the ground and Guido leaps into the fray like a whirlwind of vengeance. One assailant loses an arm to Guido's sword in a flash, another is heaved against a stone wall, the back of his skull crushed and oozing brains. The other two run for their lives.

Guido decides not to give chase. He lifts the bleeding artist onto his shoulder—he does not bother to remove the stiletto from his arm—turns, and hurries up the street. As they flee, I see that Merisi's face is a ragged, bloody mess of loose flaps of skin. Blood pours down Guido's back.

I suspect that the other assassin hired by the Tomassonis gathered a gang of thugs to help him, and that he has succeeded where I have failed. The artist could not have survived such a vicious assault and the loss of so much blood. I bang my drawn rapier against a stone wall in frustration and toss a fistful of sand into the air.

---

Many weeks later I am still in Naples, despondent, living by my wits and nearly starving. But, having a few coins left, I go to the tavern where Aldo, my local 'ear', resides. He sees me enter from across the room and motions me to his table.

'You look rather thin, my friend. What ails you?'

'I failed in my quest. The painter I sought is dead. I myself saw him murdered on the street near the Cerriglio tavern.'

He gives me a quizzical look. 'I heard about that attack. He is not dead, though he hovered on the shores of Lethe for a few weeks. Duke Colonna called in the best doctor in Naples. A miracle worker. I heard that the painter's face was a ghoul's mask. This artist will never be pretty again, but he is definitely alive and painting as usual.'

I look up at him. 'What? You joke?'

'Not at all. Rest assured that my information is trustworthy.'

I reach into my pocket and place a coin on the table between us. I walk away as if in a dream.

## ❧ THE ARTIST ❧

---

Michele spends three months recovering from his wounds, slipping in and out of fevers, sipping revivifying soups, all under Guido's watchful eye. Eventually Michele is able to stand, then to walk on Guido's arm, then to walk alone, and finally to paint. For short periods at first, then more energetically and, at last, approaching his old strength and passion, although the fevers revisit occasionally, at unexpected times.

'Guido,' he says one morning on entering his studio, 'please ask the duke if I might borrow the clearest mirror in his house.'

Guido nods, exits, and returns a short while later, a good sized, framed mirror in his hands. Michele indicates where he wants it placed, near his easel. Guido says, 'Master requests that you take good care with this mirror, for it was made in Venice at great expense.'

Michele stares at his face in the glass. 'Ah, Venice. Then it must have the powerful memory of water in it. That is good.'

'It is unusually clear,' Guido notes.

Michele begins work on a painting of David and Goliath. Not a private commission or one from a local church, but a haunting image that appeared to him, in its entirety, while he was lying near death. From his bed, he had pictured the details of the work, imagining himself painting it on the blank part of the wall before him, just beneath the crucifix. The image of the painting has not left his thoughts since then, and now that he has his strength back, he throws himself into the work.

In the painting, the boy from the Biblical story, David, holds by its hair the severed head of Goliath. He has won the battle and slain the giant. Michele paints him still gripping his sword in his right hand. *I love painting my rapier, this weapon, glowing, straight—this sword that is no different than my brush. And Goliath, the head of a man so recently dead he is just realizing it. He looks out on the world for the last time with sadness and shock.*

Michele glances into the mirror. At first, he thought he might paint his own face as that of the boy David, but something changed his mind. Now he paints himself as the face of Goliath. *What does he see, this Goliath? Out there and in here? I have painted him with eyes downcast and hooded, the mouth slack and hanging open. I have seen the heads of the executed on the Ponte Sant'Angelo—I know what a severed head looks like. I see my own death approaching and I refuse to look away. It is me death comes for, it will be my head, my eyes, my open mouth—I must look at it. I marvel.*

*I am a painter painting his own death. This mirror is so clear it is like an icy pool of water that has not been disturbed in a thousand years. I have painted my own face with as much clarity and honesty as I am able, turning away from none of its ugliness, its horror, the revulsion it prompts. In that clarity, I believe, arises the essence of beauty. I may be a monster, but I have drunk life to the full. I have no regrets.*

––––––––––

Finally, the long-awaited letter comes from Del Monte. The cardinal writes that Michele can return to Rome, kneel before His Holiness the Pope, kiss the ring, and beg forgiveness. The important and powerful Camillo Borghese, a good friend of Del Monte's, ascended to the papal throne as Pope Paul V in 1605 after the short-lived reign of Pope Leo XI. Del Monte has word that His Holiness would be favourably disposed to having all charges dropped against the artist, Michelangelo Merisi da Caravaggio, and the remission granted. Cardinal Del Monte suggests Michele should bring a few paintings as gifts for the pope and other cardinals, as appreciation for their efforts. Religious subjects only, he cautions.

––––––––––

'You will return to Rome?' Guido asks him several days later, while Michele feverishly paints. Guido has learned about the letter and noticed Michele's preparations.

'Yes. As soon as I finish one more painting.' The painting he wants to complete is for the pope himself, an image of Saint Paul with a tiny dragon from the coat of arms of the Borghese family hidden in the folds of the saint's robes.

'Will you continue to require my services?'

Michele stares at the canvas while he replies. 'Don Colonna says he wants you to stay here in Naples. Your help has been well beyond anything I could have expected. You have my unending appreciation

and gratitude. If I could bring you along to Rome, I would do so, but you are the duke's man.'

'I will remember you well, and your paintings.' Guido turns and looks out the window of the studio at Vesuvius in the distance. 'Whenever I gaze at the volcano,' he says, 'I will think of you.'

Michele laughs. 'Yes. I am glad you will have it as a reminder. On my return to Rome, I will always place an empty chair in my studio to remind me of your watchful presence.'

## ⊰ THE ASSASSIN ⊱

---

I have word that he is leaving Naples for Rome. I hope that I have not missed my chance. On his journey back, I will catch him unaware and I will finally complete my task. If not, then I will be the one running— from the Tomassonis, for they will certainly have me killed for taking their money and neglecting to deliver what I promised.

The heat is unbearable—even this early in the morning—as I wait in the thin shade of a building outside the palazzo. I keep wiping sweat from my forehead to stop it from running into my eyes and blinding me. Finally, a carriage arrives from the stables and Merisi steps out of the palazzo. He is arranging the loading of his trunk. At the last minute, before the trunk is hoisted onto the carriage, he stops the servants and opens it. He appears nervous, as if he has forgotten something. He pulls out what look like rolled up paintings. Four of them. Repacks them, ensuring they are safe.

Now he turns to Guido who waits behind him. They exchange a few words, and Guido disappears back into the palazzo. I'm elated as the carriage pulls away without Guido on board. I watch closely and, after a single turn, I know they are headed to the harbour as I suspected. I hurry through back alleys to catch up.

I arrive just as the carriage is being unloaded and the trunk carried up a gangplank onto the boat. There are too many people about to consider an attack at this moment. From my hidden vantage point, I can see that Merisi keeps his hand on the trunk as he climbs up onto the barque and disappears.

It is an easy thing to steal onto a ship, especially a three-masted barque of this size, riding low in the water, pregnant with its load. I've done it in the past, more than once, and I have no trouble this time. The important thing is to avoid the crew—I have seen only ten or so hands on board.

The crew unfurl the sails, which catch a slim breeze. Soon we are coasting northward, likely heading for Civitavecchia, the port of Rome. I am in a good hiding place on deck, between bales of cotton; I cannot be seen. The barque's square, dun-coloured sails puff out with the intermittent winds, then sag, then puff out again. I know that we will be making one stop on the way to unload goods, north of Gaeta. I learned this from an ancient sailor, too old now to crew, at the harbour before I boarded. He estimated it would take about a day and a half to two days for the boat to reach Rome's port. 'It all depends on the winds,' he said. 'At this time of year, like a beautiful wife, they can be unreliable.' He opened his toothless mouth wide, turned his head from side to side, testing the wind with his open gob. 'Yes, a little less than two days. Trust me.'

Our progress is slow as the wind is fitful, just like the old salt predicted, and not entirely in our favour, trickling in from the west. Before mid-afternoon we pass the point of Gaeta, which I can glimpse in the distance. In the bay beyond Gaeta, we catch a good tailwind and pull into the small harbour at Terracina. The sun continues achingly hot. As goods are being unloaded at Terracina—luckily not my cotton bales—the wind decides to die entirely. The air goes still. I stare at the tall palm trees by the water. Their fronds hang limp.

After a half hour of stillness, from my secret niche I see Merisi stumble down the gangplank, leaving the boat in the shimmering heat. He is like a ghost abandoning a corpse. The ship is clearly going nowhere until the wind returns, so I slip out from my hiding place and hurry to follow the painter. Perhaps I can catch him in an undefended moment, but for the time being, there are still too many people about.

As I follow, I notice that Merisi appears to be in distress, stopping frequently to wipe a rag across his face, occasionally stumbling. He stops to speak to a passerby and the man points into the town. The painter walks in that direction.

I approach the same man. 'What did that fellow ask you?'

'He wanted a doctor. His face was scarlet; looked like he was burning up. He must have fever. *Mal aria* perhaps. You know him?'

'Yes, he's a friend,' I reply and hurry on.

I follow close behind. I see Merisi stop in the middle of the scorching street and let his chin fall onto his chest. Then he stumbles off to the side of the street and sits on the ground. I come close enough that I can tell he has his eyes closed. I go for my rapier. This is my moment at last.

Just then, a stiff breeze rouses the palms. A woman slams out of a house to empty a pan of water in the street and glances at me, and Merisi opens his eyes. He notices the breeze and I can tell by the look on his face that he knows what it means. 'My paintings!' he shouts. He leaps up and starts running back toward the sailing vessel. Before I can react, he hurries right past me, eyes fixed on the distance, unaware of my presence. I note that several more residents, drawn by his shout, have come to their windows, so I cannot kill him now before their gaze. Instead, I follow. Soon we can both see that the barque is starting to pull away from the dock. The strong breeze continues; the ship is on its way out to sea. Like a madman, he scrambles down along the harbour waving his arms, shouting, 'Wait! Wait!' He hurries along the beach, still waving. The boat is pulling further and further out into the bay, heading north.

I follow the artist, who, with a sudden surge of energy, sprints with all his strength and speed along the strand. I can barely keep up. In minutes, my ragged clothes are soaked through with sweat. I stop a moment, splashing into the water to refresh myself against the heat. He pulls further away. Shaking the water from my head, I hurry after.

After a while, I spot a dog cutting across the beach, acting strangely, hopping about, twitching, chasing its tail. As I draw near, I see that the beast, a large dog with long black hair, is snarling at the air, at something invisible. At that moment, for some reason, I recall Giordano Bruno's ghost, when the powder of his bones entered my nostrils so long ago. I am no seer, but it seems a bad omen. The mongrel notices me, stops, and growls, showing its teeth. I edge toward the grassy verge of the beach, pull my sword and hold it at the ready. When the dog leaps at me, I step to the side and with all my strength, thrust my sword into his heart, dropping him dead.

Merisi is now a speck in the distance.

## ❦ THE ARTIST ❧

The sun throws needles of white gold up from the sand as Michele runs. For several hours, he pelts along the beach, seldom stopping to rest, his face dripping.

In his fevered brain, he believes he can catch the boat if the wind dies again and it drifts into shore. He will board and save his paintings and continue his journey to Rome.

His head pounds. Each thump of his feet on the sand sends sharp pains shooting up through his body and out his forehead. His eyes ache from the light, sweat pouring into them. He stumbles and falls, leaps up again and hurries on, still able to glimpse the ship in the distance, its sails against the leeched blue of the molten sky. The sun reflects off the

water and sends light piercing into him. Michele turns away and hastens further up the beach. Runs on and on.

Shrieks of gulls pierce the silence. The sun is nowhere near to setting; there is no freshness anywhere in the world to soothe him. He refuses to stop, to take the time to cool himself in the waves nearby. *In this summer heat, the water must be warm as blood. I must catch the boat, I must.*

His thirst is unbearable. The sun pounds on his head relentlessly. He vomits onto his chest and doesn't stop running.

*Where am I?* He has passed out and pitched forward, face down on the sand. He rolls over and stares into the sharp glare of the sun. *My paintings.* Someone comes and casts a shadow over him.

*Who is that? That face. I know that face. Is it . . . is it Luca? What are you doing here? My paintings, Luca, I must get my paintings. Help me.* Michele believes he is speaking out loud but is unsure. In his fevered state, he has forgotten entirely about Luca's attack in the palazzo.

Luca gazes into Michele's eyes, which are all sky, and glimpses there a reflection of himself. Michele reaches up.

Luca, one hand holding his sword high, instinctively extends his other hand to help.

———

He is still alive in the light that falls on the world.

# ⊰ ACKNOWLEDGEMENTS ⊱

I would like to thank my hard-working and perspicacious editor for the press, Stephanie Small, as well as proofing editor, Martin Llewellyn. Thanks to Tim Inkster, publisher of Porcupine's Quill, for his creative additions of beautiful images to my books. Thanks also to a number of people who offered editorial suggestions: Nicola Vulpe, Diane Schoemperlen, and my favourite editor of all, Faith Seltzer. My apologies if I have forgotten anyone.

I am grateful to the Ontario Arts Council for several grants during the writing of this book.

Interior images are after engravings from *Picturesque Europe* published by Cassell, Petter & Galpin, London, 1879.

---

Mark Frutkin is the author of over a dozen books of fiction, non-fiction and poetry. His works include the Trillium Book Award-winning *Fabrizio's Return* (Vintage, 2006), which was shortlisted for the Commonwealth Writers' Prize for Best Book, and *Atmospheres Apollinaire* (The Porcupine's Quill, 1988), which was shortlisted for the Governor General's Award, the Trillium and the Ottawa Book Award. His latest book, *Where Angels Come to Earth* (Longbridge Books, 2020), with Toronto photographer, Vincenzo Pietropaolo, presents a visual and poetic appreciation of Italian culture. He lives in Ottawa.